# Ahead of the Shadows

A.B. Kyazze

Humanity in the Landscape Publishing

This edition first published in 2022 by Humanity in the Landscape Publishers

86-90 Paul Street, London EC2A 4NE

www.humanitylandscape.co.uk

ISBN (eBook): 978-1-7395908-1-9
ISBN (Paperback): 978-1-7395908-0-2

## Dedication

To KMSK, who changed my world completely
when he came into it.

# Part 1

# One

## Bene

### Funchal Airport, Madeira, Portugal, 21 June 2022

From his small oval window Bene can't see Aunt Magda anymore. She must have stepped out of sight when he boarded the plane. He wonders if she is sad or relieved to be left alone again after all these years. He tightens the grey nylon seatbelt around his waist. The pilot starts the engines and the plane glides back from the terminal. It pivots slowly, and he can see the mountains of Madeira revolve away.

The plane takes off and then tracks a course to the mainland. He strains backwards to see the port. The familiar streets and rocky volcanoes of the island shrink into the distance. His eyes are drawn to the sea, wind whipping up the waves. It would be a good day for surfing. The wind is offshore and the waves are rolling in perfectly. He has never been far from this coast in his whole life. He knows its smells, its rhythms and seasons. He doesn't know anything else.

He takes out his sketch pad and favourite pencil and starts to draw his right hand with his left. Despite the small bumps and jerks as the plane gains altitude, the drawing is half decent. He always comes back to this old exercise as a warm up. Gives him a chance to centre his thoughts. His first sketch is of a clenched fist, from the side. The drawing looks like the whorl of a snail shell, and he quickly turns the page for a different one. This time, a more relaxed hand, with the same cracks and lines and chickenpox scars that he's always drawn. The engines get louder and he wonders what the pilot is doing. If he concentrates enough on getting the shading and curves just right, maybe he won't think about the chances of this little propeller plane falling out of the sky.

He forgot to check how long this flight to Lisbon is. Is there food? Probably not, on this kind of plane. Then he has another, larger plane to Paris, and a third one to Nairobi. At seventeen, he pretends he is a world traveller, but he has never been on a plane by himself before. Come to think of it, he's never been in a different country than Mum, before now.

It wasn't supposed to be this way. Mum had planned it as a surprise, a trip for them both to go to Kenya as a reward for his passing his exams. But then she got the call about her old friend Lucian's emergency surgery in London, and she hastily changed the plan. Bene had to go on ahead, or else they would have lost the money on both tickets. She would come later, as soon as she was sure that Lucian had pulled through.

Bene runs his hands over the seams and wrinkles of the envelope Mum gave him. He doesn't know what to expect, but it isn't this. Photos tumble out and he spreads them onto his tray table. There aren't many, just seven. He lines up the edges, but they're not all the same size so it's a bit haphazard. Some are faded and look like they were printed a long time ago. Others look newly printed but from old negatives. The black and white ones have rough edges. He can tell that Mum cut them herself with the guillotine in the darkroom. In all of them the same black man is framed from different angles. In most of the photos he is with other people, and he seems to be tall. He is bald, and has an air of authority. People would probably think he was

4

handsome. In one of them he is talking to people, pointing at something in the distance. Seems to be someone who explains things. Probably a good leader – that's what he looks like.

In another photo he is in a large group shot. Black, white and Asian people are in it, a real mix. The lighting is harsh – must be direct sun – and all the white people are squinting or holding up an arm to shade their eyes from the glare. But not him. He is proud and African and not bothered in the slightest. But he's not really smiling either. Not a real smile. More of a grim expression. He looks a bit stressed, to be honest.

In only one photo does he actually look happy, and it's not a black and white handprinted one. It's got faded colour, and you can tell it's old because Mum is in it as a young woman. She's got this long braid like a hippy and there's no trace of grey in her hair. Her face is like a girl's; he almost doesn't recognise her. She's looking at the man from the side, her mouth slightly open with a laugh. He also is happy, but it's more subtle. Like he's just told a joke that others may take a little while to catch on to. Mum's got it, though, she's always quick like that.

The man looks directly at the camera, with a cheeky knowing look, and it's the eyes that do it. Nothing else really looks that much like Bene, but there's something there.

But does that make a man a father?

No. He's still just a stranger.

# Lena

### Malanje, Angolan Highlands, May 2002

It looked like how she remembered. Dry, dusty highlands with the colours of the land muted and subtle. Mile after mile with few signs of life. Just the parallel sets of hill tracks you could see from the plane, the marks left behind by the tyres of the lorries that crossed the distances to deliver relief aid to the camps. And the marks from the armoured vehicles, delivering soldiers to the outpost towns in the provinces to provide security, as promised in the peace accords.

It was a bizarre time, the end of a war. So many pledges were made by governments and officials. Hundreds of thousands of displaced people needed urgent humanitarian relief. The UN was involved at all levels. The airport was full of planes from the World Food Programme, and lorries with large loads linked together left the hangar at all hours. It was a strange thing to witness. Stranger still trying to make sense of it. Maybe she'd lost the habit of close observation, the constant learning and decision making that comes with being a photographer in a conflict zone.

She chided herself: it had only been three months away, after all. The weeks of feeling the intense fevers and sickness, and then the slow recovery. Malaria was a grisly disease. She was grateful to be done with it. She'd had a mild case, the consultant had said, shaking his head at the consequences of her going off her malaria medicine that time. Even though it was just for a night or two. It was unplanned, unsafe and had consequences.

But she had recovered, and now she was on her way back. To a man she loved. Yes, it felt right, saying that to herself. And a job – a real, salaried job! At the age of twenty-four, she finally felt that she had a purpose. She was to be a full-time communications officer. For the international aid organisation Community Water Angola, run by Kojo Appiah. They would have to figure out the proper management structure, she supposed. Everything would be strictly professional, in public.

Would it be the same between them? After their intense time just as the war ended, she'd had to be evacuated because of her high fevers. Since then, there had been phone calls, but that was not the same as being in the same place, living through things together.

Kojo's letters on thin airmail stationery had found her in the UK when she came out of hospital. His handwriting was unfamiliar, but he wrote with the same rhythms and mannerisms as his speech: formal, self-effacing and calm. He was a close observer of other people and shifts in dynamics. Humour laced through the words, even when the meaning was serious – about their work providing water, sanitation and health clinics to displacement camps throughout the north of Angola.

She remembered what they had shared, and the details of the humanitarian work. But when she was back in London, that life seemed utterly foreign. She couldn't explain it to her old friends, even ones like Lucian who had known her all her life.

Did she have all Kojo's letters? Six had arrived, haphazardly spaced so she never knew when to expect one. She wanted to ask him if there were any that had gone astray. She had been so thirsty for news about him, about their friends there, and the team.

She had written too, when she was strong enough. When her brain regained the clarity needed to form sentences, to think about how her words might be received so far away. But at first, she couldn't. Not when the fever had burnt out all her energy. When sitting up was a struggle, and blinking felt like a chore. She remembered closing her eyes and resting her vision. Awake, and still sensing things around her, but with the shutters down. Then there was no longer any responsibility to process visual information. For a photographer, it was a surprise that at the height of her sickness the main feeling when her eyes were closed was relief.

Now, it was the opposite. She couldn't wait to see his face again, to start taking photos, to be useful and back in the action. She didn't want to miss a thing. Adrenaline flowed through her and her attention was heightened to the details. She recognised the smells of the small plane, burning up fuel on the approach to Malanje, the scent of sweat on the worn leather strap of her camera bag. Out of the window she saw the edges of the frontier town coming into view. The dark stripe of the matted dirt runway was up ahead.

She was re-entering a tricky post-war context. Like all the aid workers, she would have to do the dance of the unpredictable. She was determined to make a success of this. She would never forget her pills or her mosquito repellent again, not for anybody.

# Two

## Bene

### Paris, 21 June 2022

This is really going to be a challenge. What was Mum thinking, booking him a night alone in a Paris youth hostel? She always has such faith in him. Maybe too much. She treats him as if he is capable of anything, without stopping to ask if he can actually manage. She should have come. Or maybe given him a ticket for one of his friends. That would've been more fun. On his own, his schoolboy French isn't very good. He can read street signs and ask for a croque-monsieur and that's about it. Not nearly as good as his English and Portuguese, of course.

The hostel seems alright, though. It's an international chain with bright signs and an all-night vending machine. There are kids about his age hanging about reception, not looking too shady. Probably backpacking across Europe or something. He'd like to do that with friends sometime, maybe next year after he finds out if he gets into uni or not.

He takes a top bunk in a room for six, but it doesn't seem like the other people will show. Or maybe they will come as a group, and he'll be the odd one out. He doesn't want to stick around to see. He would much prefer to be on the move, not waiting around to be scrutinised.

He packs away his suitcase in the locker, taking with him only his backpack with his camera, sketchbook and important papers: the tickets, his passport and Mum's letter. If the hostel goes up in flames or something, he will still be able to keep going.

It's a warm night, but not hot. He'll be okay in jeans and a t-shirt. He catches a view of his reflection in the storefront glass on the way out. He knows he hunches his shoulders; he can't help it. He's tall; people always think he's at least a couple of years older than he is. His short twists are still holding, just. The air was so dry on the plane, they might fuzz out. Funny thing, being half-Ghanaian and never been to Ghana or anywhere in Africa. He has always expected Mum to take him there, and instead she's sending him off on his own, without a clue.

With Mum, it never serves to ask directly about the past. You have to do it gradually, maybe while looking at photographs, or if a news item comes on the telly. You have to let her tell you things in her own rhythm. Years ago, he realised he had to keep his own reactions in check if he wanted to get any information out of her. He feels like he understands her now, and since she is half of his genes, that means he comes closer to understanding himself. That's better than it is for a lot of people, he figures. It's just that there are pieces missing.

Usually, they don't have to say much when the two of them are together. But other times they are both bursting with reactions to a headline or a work of art and they stumble over each other. That's what can happen, he reckons, with a single mum and an only child. The connection runs deep, an odd symmetry. But that doesn't mean that everything has been said, because it hasn't.

He sees a poster announcing *La Fête de la Musique, le 21 juin 2022.* He knows what the words mean – a music festival. But what is it? And where? It could be cool. He should check it out.

He feels like a tourist, and shrinks further into his shoulders. He knows, from growing up in Funchal, there's a clear divide between people who know, and the tourists who have no clue. Those who have done the research, and have the books and the maps, they know even less than the others. They don't know what they don't know. The local reasons and rhythms and things – you can't translate that. And you can't read about it. You just have to live it.

Will people know he's a stranger here? He keeps his head down. He looks at his trainers – quite beaten up. He wishes he had brought that brimmed hat he left back home. It would have been perfect here. But sometimes strangers get weird about brown-skinned boys wearing hats. Make all sorts of assumptions about them, read too much into it, whether it's a woolly hat or a broad brim or a baseball cap like the Americans. Like they would instantly rob them or something. It's like, chill out, people! It's just a hat.

But he can't say that, not to the strangers who give him that look. He may not know the language so well, but he knows that look. Those who slip a hand to check that their bag is zipped closed before he passes by. When he sees people like that, if he does happen to be wearing his hat, he likes to raise a hand to it, like a gentleman in the old days. Sometimes he even stops to say something to strangers that they wouldn't expect. That's the great thing about that brimmed hat. You put that on your head and you can trick people, do anything at all.

Last time he wore that hat, he surprised a couple – just off a cruise ship, you could tell in a second. He tipped it up and said to the woman: 'Good day to you, m'lady!' Using the poshest kind of British accent. The tourists had no clue it was fake. Sunburnt and sweaty, clothes clinging to all the wrong places in the heat. But their faces transformed, just with a tip of a hat and a fake accent. People can be so funny about strangers. They struggle to hide their initial reaction, and then try to overdo it with the niceness. He can't stand it. He walked away quick as he could after that.

He holds a picture of the map of Paris in his head. His memory is good in that way, like a camera. A few seconds looking at something and bam, it's there for him when he needs it. In his mind, he can travel the map, twist it in space and see where he needs to go. There's something spatial to his memory, and he's only recently realised other people don't have it – Mum, for example. It's quite hard to describe to her the way his brain works. It's something like seeing all three dimensions of anything, whenever you need it. No matter which way you look at it, you know there's a depth or distance to it. You can just turn it around in your head.

He starts to run, to get the blood flowing and work some of the kinks out of his legs from the plane journey. Some heads turn as he goes by, his backpack banging softly against his back, but he's moving too fast to care. He imagines himself a blur flying past the students and the tourists and the snooty women with the tiny dogs. He wants to explore – doesn't need anyone's approval to do that. He's chasing the daylight, and today, the longest day of the year, he has all the time in the world.

He tries to remember when sunset is. Sometime after ten, he's sure of that. Paris must be pretty safe after dark, he figures. It looks so manicured and perfect. He can't imagine that they'd let it get rough. He follows the diagonal Boulevard Saint-Germain until he cuts left and arrives at what looks like a country castle all out of place on the corner of busy Paris streets. He submits to a bag search, shows his student ID card and ducks inside the Rodin Museum. As he promised Mrs Penani, perhaps the oldest, and definitely the best, art teacher his school has ever had, he has come to pay homage to the great sculptor himself.

The place is surprisingly small, and it is clear you are expected to spend most of your time in the gardens. He takes out his sketchbook in front of *The Thinker*. Seeing it in person is so much better than in the books. The muscular legs are thick and folded. You can see the sinews straining underneath. The face, buried in thought, brooding. The hands, something about the hands bothers him. They seem slightly too large. But who is he to criticise a master? Must be about a sense of perspective, or emphasising a point. Hands mean so many different things to people. And they are really difficult to do.

Bene's choice of material wouldn't be clay, he has to admit. Although he isn't bad at it, his ideal is more industrial and abstract. He likes working with metal or blunt, heavy materials. Strong lines. Edges say something to people, like a knife, they show power, danger and a direction of travel. And scale. He can do large – that's his trademark. He'd like to go even bigger. Sculpt pieces that throw people into the shadows, make them shrink back and contemplate just how tiny we all are.

Gil takes the piss out of him, though. Thinks his work is compensating for something. Like Gil knows anything. Sometimes it's a pain in the arse to have a friend like Gil. Always criticising. Popping the balloons of other people's inspiration, just for a laugh. He's not even sure why they are friends, just always have been. They are the only two mixed-race kids in the class; everyone just expects them to be best mates.

He's glad not to have anyone around who knows him, after all. He smiles as he looks up at the wind twisting the leaves, teasing summer out of the shade. He can be whoever he likes, for this one night in Paris.

# Lena

### Malanje, Angola, May 2002

The mosquito net fluttered with some changes in the atmosphere of the room. She lay next to Kojo and listened to his breathing. He lay on his back, no shirt. He always slept in a wrap around the waist, said that it helped him relax and reminded him of his childhood. She could make out the West African patterns in the fabric, and she liked to play gently with it while he slept.

His eyes were closed. She loved how calm he was. And the trust that he had in her, to allow her to watch him while he slept. Defences were down, and his face was gentle, despite the shadow of stubble under his cheekbones. Even in sleep he still held some lines around the eyes and mouth. Years of being so serious had left marks, times when he forgot how to laugh. He'd told her about the conditions in refugee camps in Kenya and Sudan, but since she hadn't lived through them, she just had to listen. When he was like this, lying next to her, it was hard to remember him as anything but safe and tender.

She rolled over to put her arm across his chest and wrap a leg across his hips. He made a small moan, halfway between sleep and wakefulness. She rubbed her hand over his collarbone. She liked to imagine painting him with clay or warm oil. They had never had the chance to do the normal things that lovers do, like go for a massage or take a holiday together somewhere with palm trees. And yet, that didn't matter. She played with the soft sensation of his chest hair, then took her hand down towards his navel.

He smiled, and moved his hand to hers. So he wasn't asleep, not yet.

'You don't want to sleep,' he said, keeping his eyes closed.

'There's so much to catch up on,' she said.

'Making love, you mean?' He opened his eyes and pulled her into a straddle on top of him. 'Again?'

'Yes... and other things. I want to know what you've been doing, what you've been thinking about...'

'You know all that. It's just been work, alongside Brad and Jeanette and the whole team. Work and coordination meetings with the UN, and orientation briefings for new agencies setting up... I've not thought of anything else for so long...'

He sat up halfway, braced on his elbows. 'And you, of course. I lost a lot of sleep over you.'

'Is that so?' She twirled her finger around his navel.

He smiled. 'You know it's true.'

'If you were so worried, why didn't you come to London to see me?'

'I told you, didn't you get that letter?' She had, but she wanted to hear it directly from his lips. 'The UK embassy would not grant me an emergency visa. You have to be married for that. And the application time for a non-urgent visa was twelve weeks. When I knew you were out of danger and coming back, it didn't make sense.'

She pushed him back down, his shoulders against the pillows. 'But you would have come, if I was really in danger?'

'Of course. You know I would have found a way.'

She had told him about her time in the hospital and her fuzzy memories of the fevers. He'd listened attentively, although he and all the others had had malaria before. Everyone who worked in the field did at some point.

'You're on the mend now, though.' He played with her hips, tracing the curve of her thigh while they spoke.

'Better than ever,' she said.

'Ready to start the new job? We really missed you out here.'

'As a photographer? Or as your girlfriend?'

He laughed and rolled her over onto her back. 'One of those positions isn't paid, I'm afraid. We have to uphold certain moral standards here. I hope you understand, Miss Rodrigues.'

'It's *Ms* Rodrigues to you, thank you very much.' She kissed him on the tip of the nose for emphasis, like a full stop.

'Why the change in title?'

'I'm a modern woman. A paid photojournalist now. Show some respect!'
She reached behind for a pillow and whacked him with it. They laughed
and whispered and kissed. It was funny, how easily they could fall into their
own familiar, yet still unexpected, kind of intimacy.

She didn't tell him about the bleeding. He didn't ask, and she didn't feel
like it was ever the right pause in the conversation to say.

All gone now, in any case. Not even worth thinking about. It wasn't
anything anyway. Just a potential that didn't happen.

# Three

## Bene

First time in Paris, you have to see it. The Eiffel Tower is barricaded off for security reasons, and the tourists are queueing to squeeze through the barriers. He doesn't feel the need to go to the top. He views it from the grass where he sits back, resting his head on his backpack, and admires the wrought iron.

It's a very pleasing structure, to his mind. The way that the straight beams give the impression of being curved has an industrial kind of grace. He promised to buy Gil a keyring. He lies back and shuts his eyes.

He thinks of Gil and the other kids – what are they doing to celebrate the end of exams? They'll probably be out surfing and partying. But quite a few will be getting jobs working in cafés or catering to the cruise ships coming into port. Gil will probably be talking up some millionaire old lady, trying to fleece her for all she's got. Selling ballroom dance lessons or something. Funny that guy. He can talk a diamond ring off someone's finger, if he tries hard enough.

Bene isn't like that. Maybe that's why Gil sticks with him. The quiet guy is the ultimate cover – Gil could talk the volume for both of them. But he doesn't mind, not too much. You need to have mates, after all.

He hears guitar strumming, something like the old songs that Mum used to play. He looks around and sees a circle of kids, huddled around a guy with a guitar. Are they his age? Older, he reckons, looking at how comfortable they are with their bottles of wine in the open. Nothing to hide. No one keeping track of them or when they have to be home. The guys are letting their hair grow. The girls have long skirts, the tie-dyed lumpy ones so you can't see the shape of their legs. But on top they have teeny feminine tops, flat stomachs showing. Guess some people find that a turn-on; not for him, though.

One girl looks over at him and smiles while she flips her blonde hair behind her shoulder. She has a nose piercing connected by a gold chain to a cuff on her ear. It's huge and gaudy, he can see it from this distance. Not his type. He swivels around to put his back to the guitar player, and faces the Eiffel Tower once more.

He takes out his notebook, and quickly works on a sketch of the southwest leg of the tower. He likes how sturdy it looks, like an elephant standing strong. He doesn't feel that he has to draw the whole tower, just one leg is enough to concentrate on and really try to get right. He's glad he brought the charcoal, it's the right medium for this, for sure. The only problem is getting the grey on your hands when you blur the shadows. Can't be helped.

'*Ce n'est pas mal,*' comes a voice from behind him. He is annoyed to be distracted, doesn't look away from his sketchbook.

The one with the nose-chain sits down next to him and puts her legs out straight. Her feet are bare and muddy. It's like she has been walking all day, but it couldn't be a regular thing because otherwise she didn't look homeless. She probably normally has shoes.

'Sorry, what?' he says, pretending he doesn't understand.

'*Tu n'est pas d'ici?*' she asks. He shakes his head, pointing to his ears as if they're not working properly.

'Are you Bree-teesh?' she asks, more enthusiastic than before.

'Sort of. Not really.'

She looks confused.

'Half,' he says, gesturing to his short twists. 'British-Portuguese, actually. And the other half Ghanaian.'

She lifts her shoulders and grins, as if she hasn't met anyone this exciting all year.

'*Fala português?*' he asks, expecting a no.

She continues to grin and shakes her head, making the nose-chain ensemble jingle.

He keeps drawing. She watches, leaning over so that she is close to his arm. He feels her body heat and smells an earthy kind of perfume. Is that weed? Her friends have switched to a new song. It's in French and they are singing the chorus together with gusto.

Without warning, she kisses him on the cheek and stands up. She then lifts her arms to the sky. '*T'as du talent!*' she declares and gives a loud laugh, like she has just won something in a competition. She swirls her skirt around her legs, walking and turning at the same time. She moves in a vague path back to her friends. '*Vraiment un artiste...*'

He doesn't know whether he should watch or ignore her. But it doesn't matter; she seems like she's in her own hippy world. It's nice that she thinks he's an artist, even if she is a bit kooky. In his peripheral vision he sees her stop a bit away from her group and start pivoting. Eyes shut, big closed-lipped smile on her face, she starts a repetitive dance in one spot. Kick and quarter-turn. Kick and quarter-turn. Smile and swing. She seems to take huge pleasure in the movement, in the air around her, in the music or whatever else is on her mind.

Probably on E, he thinks. He's never tried it, but Gil has. Too risky, to his mind. Could make you feel fantastic for a moment, but some people take it and are never normal again. He heard of one girl who took it and then her inner organs filled up with water and she drowned, just like that. Inside her own body.

# Lena

### Malanje, Angola, June 2002

They had settled into a rhythm. A hectic one, fuelled by coffee and adrenaline, with timing dictated by the sun, and the pattern of coordination briefings, press visits, and vehicle convoys leaving and coming back. CWA had a huge caseload of projects to deliver. Tens of thousands of displaced people were relying on CWA for water, sanitation and basic health care. Even with the end of the war and the arrival of more agencies and staff from across the continent, there was always much more work to be done than people to do it. Kojo had seen this before, when he worked in Operation Lifeline Sudan and the Kakuma camps in northern Kenya. He explained the different coordination structures, and the various agencies of the UN, Red Cross, and others. He introduced Lena to colleagues he knew from years past, different emergencies in various places.

Lena started to get used to the language of the humanitarian relief, talking about 'sit-reps' (situation reports), 'IDPs' (displaced people), and 'wat-san' (water and sanitation). Some big names in the media came through Malanje and wanted to hear her views on the situation. But she almost never went on camera herself; she was much happier providing the photos and supporting someone else as spokesperson making the points on live camera to the wider world.

She wasn't trying to impress people or make new friends. For the first time in her life, she really felt that there was a strong reason to get up in the morning, because her photographs could be of use, helping people. She had a direct link with the BBC, AFP, CNN, *The New York Times* and others. They took her digital uploads whenever there was a decent enough satellite connection. Otherwise, she used the international pouches for the rolls of film, hearing back in a week or two from head office if the shots were of any use.

Here she was fast and decisive. There was no time to hesitate. She ran on instinct. She just knew what would make a good shot or worthwhile photo essay. It was often the telling detail that would capture the wider story, about war and displacement and humanitarian need. Sometimes it was the small possessions that people managed to hold onto, despite being moved from place to place with nearly nothing.

One of her favourite moments was when she was invited into a small shack on the edge of a displacement camp. The place was made of thin planks holding up the roof, with gaps you could see through. But it was a home. There was a calendar from 1998 on one wall, advertising orange Fanta. The mother opened a small drawer to pull out a tiny bundle wrapped in tissue. Inside were letters and two photographs, unframed and unprotected. One was from an earlier generation, and the woman gestured that the baby held on the lap of a stern-faced father was her own mother. The other one was of the woman, sitting and smiling with lips closed, in front of a man wearing an Angolan army uniform. It was a formal studio portrait, black and white with a plain sheet for background. A tall boy, standing next to his father, was serious and determined. Another younger brother, also standing, was smirking and looking outside the frame.

Sitting on the bench next to the mother were two girls in white dresses, smiling and looking like they wanted to please. A baby was clasped on her lap, wide-eyed, unsmiling and unable to make sense of the strange moment, frozen in time. The woman gestured that she did not know where the father or the eldest boy were, but she was lucky to have the other children with her, even if all they had for a home was this shack with gaps in the walls that let the sand and the wind through. Lena took a photo of the woman holding the two historical pictures.

When Lena was back at the CWA villa, she printed out a copy, and pinned it next to her bed. It meant a lot to her, when people shared photographs that they treasured, marking family and time.

Kojo understood this about her, her dedication to photography, and her full immersion in the work. There was a sense of satisfaction in having defeated any indecision. And not needing to ask permission to do a job well. She fit in with the team, in a way that she had never done before. Working sixteen- to eighteen-hour days, she would fall asleep deeply, but wake up with no struggle. Gone were nights of tossing and turning, when the luxury of insomnia meant that sleep was an option, not really a necessity. Here she slept like she drank water – it was a deep thirst, and rejuvenated her in a way that she had never felt before.


'Promotion?' Lena asked. 'What are you talking about?'

'For me, and for you as well,' Kojo said.

'I don't understand. I just got here.'

'Months ago... I know, the timing is a bit quick. But in NGO work it sometimes happens like that. CWA are finally giving me acknowledgement for years of service. I've been in this country so long, Lena, you wouldn't believe. It's great news.' He sounded almost apologetic. 'And they needed a regional comms officer too. There's been a gap for a while now.'

'You want to live in Nairobi?'

'I'll be responsible for the whole East and Southern Africa region. For Community Water Worldwide – the global arm. It's a real step up for me.'

'I've never been there.'

'There's a lot of opportunity for travel, covering Angola, Congo, Sudan, Kenya... you'll love it.'

'We'll still be together?'

'Sure we will. Most of the time. Although I'll have to attend board meetings and things with donors. Tedious stuff. You'll be having more adventures than I will.'

She nodded, not adjusting yet her fixed ideas of what she had flown back to Angola to accomplish. Everything she had started to build up – the friendships, the contacts, the respect she'd gained from some good coverage of her photo essays in the international press. Would that follow her across to East Africa?

'Think of all the photos you'll be able to take! It's your chance to show the world what's going on, places journalists are too afraid to go. It's a once-in-a-lifetime chance, Lena.'

'What about the team here in Malanje? There's still so much to do.'

'You'll rotate back here for comms work, and still have your connections. I'll be one level higher, so I will still have oversight of the Angola programme. But there will be a new Angola country director; they'll recruit for my replacement as soon as I accept the position.'

He looked so happy, she had to be pleased for him. That's why they were a good couple – they understood each other's work patterns and goals without question.

He held out his arms to her, and she came in for a hug. 'You and me,' he said, 'we're regional staff now.'

She wasn't used to the idea, but that was okay. She figured she still had the same cameras, the same determination to get the story out, just a wider remit. If anything, the challenge had grown much bigger. If he thought she could do it, she was game.

'Where are we going first?' she asked. 'Kenya?'

'Congo.'

## Goma, Democratic Republic of Congo, July 2002

The end of the runway had been destroyed by lava, left in thick raised strips that stretched out like fossilised tree roots. Lena had never seen anything like that before. It was as if the black lava had swallowed the colour and obliterated all light, leaving no chance of a reflection. Even the shadows were masked and absorbed.

No passenger or supply planes were allowed to land in Goma after the eruption of Mount Nyiragongo in January. The helicopter pilot pointed to where the flows had nearly reached Lake Kivu. 'It could have caused a poison cloud!' he shouted over the noise of the engine. 'Like Cameroon in '86.'

The beat-beat-beat of the rotor blades above shook the helicopter as she leaned towards the window to take photographs. She clipped her camera to the nylon harness that held her in place, so it could not fall out of her hands. But the tangle of straps also made composition tricky. If she tried to get photos without the nylon straps or the metal of the helicopter crowding in on the shot, she had to crop in tightly. Instead, she used the curved edge of the helicopter door to frame the scene below.

It was too loud to speak, and in any case Kojo was intent on learning everything he could from the bird's-eye view they were granted before they came in to land. She looked out at a scene shaped by the force of the eruption. Kojo had only time to quickly explain about the recent volcanic eruption, and the mass displacement that followed in an area already impacted by an ongoing civil war. She would have to gather more information on the go, filling in the blanks later as needed.

The photographer in her appreciated the beauty and starkness of the landscape. In the viewfinder she captured the path of the lava flow from the peak, twenty kilometres away. Streaks of black rock spilled out and were now solid, sloped along a downhill trajectory, towards the town and pointing to the lake. The dormant cone of the volcano after the eruption looked like a charred stump. She had been warned that it could blow again at any time.

Away from the lava flow, there were groves with the shaggy fronds of banana trees. Somehow their roots had avoided being singed in the eruption, and they were thriving, taking in all the light and nutrients they could absorb.

Alongside and on top of the lava, there were buildings resurrected in new layers, with new paint and new colours. They were perched, with little regard to perpendicular lines, where the new ground allowed them to settle. Some showed remnants of the shacks below, half-buried up to their windows in the eruption. Haphazard shop signs called out opportunities for buying SIM cards or jerry cans for water or fuel.

From the air, she could see women squatting by the side of the damaged runway with baskets of vegetables and fruit. The colours jumped out at the camera in the sunlight, defying the blackness that had swallowed everything just six months before. So many different shades of red, orange, yellow and green – Lena couldn't name all the produce, but it cheered her to know that plants were growing back, even from this damaged environment. Trucks, cars and 4x4s bumped over the uneven surface of the solidified lava. A pickup truck, the back filled to capacity with people, boxes and chicken cages, crested across the intersection of a new road and the lava flow.

As the helicopter came in to land, the thump of the propellers grew slower but the machine still vibrated and shook. They hovered over a circle in a field. The grass rippled in waves from the wind. With the jolt of the landing Lena nearly dropped her camera, but she held on with both hands, forearms wrapped around the nylon harness. She watched through the window as the tips of the blades began to slow down their blur, and then the pilot unsnapped his harness, opened the door and released the ladder.

'We made it!' Kojo leapt out of his seat and climbed down.

She felt unsteady despite the machine being safely on the ground. She took a few breaths before unclipping her harness and gathering up her camera bag and backpack.

Kojo strode out ahead of her with his arm outstretched, ready to shake the hand of a Congolese staff member, a smiling tall guy wearing a CWW t-shirt. Shifting his backpack to the other shoulder, Kojo nodded and removed his sunglasses, looking in the faces of his new staff, eager to get to know their names and roles individually. He did not look back to Lena to say anything or gauge her impression of the place. He did not need her assessment.

That night, they were lodged in separate rooms.

Lena looked through the pictures on the back of her digital camera. She was still learning how to get the best images out of it, having had it only a few months. She wasn't sure if the black and whites were as strong as they would be in classic negative film. Here they looked unimpressive and grey. It was frustrating, the inability to translate what she witnessed into this new format: how black it really was, this frozen evidence of a devastating volcano. She vowed to have both cameras – the film camera and the digital one – ready at all times to better show both black depths and white highlights, as well as the full range of colour. The landscape was so dramatic, and the story was a strong one: *refugee camps threatened by lava; rebuilding despite the challenges*. She didn't want to miss her chance for the defining shot.

The hotel was modest with no air conditioning. At dinner she sat apart from Kojo, making new acquaintances and asking about their work. She had her notebook out and scribbled down ideas of what might be useful for later photographs, when she got to see projects. She asked them what they wanted to show, how she could be of service to the programme on the ground. They tried to describe what they wanted documented and shared with donors and the media far away.

Occasionally she would look up and see him. Kojo's meal was only half eaten as he leaned forward to listen and brought a range of people across the table into the same conversation. He was already fulfilling the regional director role as leader, facilitator, listener, and friend, acting as he had for years in Angola. He could bring out the knowledge in people, to serve a higher level of analysis that the whole team could share. Other times he leaned back and drummed his fingertips on the surface of the table, and she knew he was searching for the right word. She couldn't hear the answer but she knew when he had found it because his face burst into a smile and then he laughed hard, whether at himself or at the story, she couldn't say. His cheerfulness rang around the table and she had to smile too. He was in his element, and that made everyone around him at ease and able to share in his steady feeling.

After dinner, most of the team retired early so she did as well. All except Kojo and the local team leader in Goma, who continued to talk over beers in the hotel bar. She didn't mind if she wasn't there at his side. Her purpose here was to document the relief effort, and bring the human experiences to life in pictures. She would use photography to tell the stories of what people had been through, and the impact the humanitarian assistance was making. Even if people had never seen Congo or would not have the chance to come, they would see her pictures and have a sense of what it felt like to be there.

The noise of an occasional car went past her shuttered window. She wondered who would be travelling after dark in this place. It was technically still a conflict zone, despite signs of normal life taking root around the town. Before the volcano, Congo's war was centred here in the east, with militias of different loyalties fighting and vying for power, then disappearing into the bush. This left the population traumatised and living in a constant state of fear. The volcanic eruption seemed to pause the fighting for some months, as the terrain had changed and jungle had burned away somewhat, leaving the town calmer than it had been in years. But people said that fighting could return any time, if not to Goma then to a village or unprotected town in the bush nearby.

A loud rumble moved past her windows. It sounded like a heavily loaded lorry or maybe an armoured vehicle. The noise stayed too long, as if it was struggling to get past this modest row of guest houses. Perhaps the road had been narrowed by the path of the lava. She didn't know the situation here, could be anything or nothing. Lena tried to ignore it and not worry.

She took her malaria medicine and pulled the netting around the bed. Lying on her back with a torch, she shifted through the sit-reps that were shared as part of her briefing, trying to keep straight the numbers of refugees and their settings. There were so many different acronyms of various armed groups and aid agencies active in Eastern Congo, she needed to gain some sense of the history and timeline. She was also learning about the involvement of foreign armies – Rwandan, Ugandan, Angolan armies had all meddled in Congo's war. UN peacekeepers were here too, although not very successful in keeping the peace, it seemed. This was no simple natural disaster; it was a humanitarian response to a devastating volcanic eruption on top of a complicated civil war that had never really stopped for the past six years.

She was aware her reading provided just a cursory understanding, but the details were important, and she wanted to commit the important dates and figures to memory. This job was the closest she had come yet to having a profession, and she didn't want to mess it up.

Even though her head was pressed against the mosquito net, she sat up and unfolded a map out on the bedspread, showing Goma and the surrounding districts. They were in an area called 'The Kivus': North Kivu and South Kivu, two of the most actively contested areas in a country that had been locked in civil war since 1996. She was due to head northeast to Bunia, a side trip without Kojo. He didn't have the time to go deep into the field when he still had to see his new office in Nairobi and meet the regional staff. She wondered how it would feel to be in the field without him. In Angola, they had always been together. They'd had different jobs to do and might not have seen each other during the day, but they were part of the same team. They had shared their observations and reflections, making sense of the different pieces of work. It was an odd feeling to be planning to go ahead on her own.

She tried to shake off her worries. She would see him soon enough in Nairobi, of course. There she would download the digital images and develop the black and white negative film, picking out the best photos to demonstrate CWW's work and the humanitarian need.

After she turned off the light, she had little desire to sleep. Her eyes sought patterns and subtle movements of light in the dark. The rotating fan quietly pushed the cone of the hanging mosquito net back and forth. It should have lulled her to sleep, but the feeling of intermittent cool only made her feel more alert.

Congo scared her in a way that Angola had not. It was different than when she first arrived in the field in Angola. Then, she didn't have access to the sit-reps and the security assessments. She had been naïve. Her mission had only been to look for her late sister DJ, without any idea of what was going on below the surface.

She hated that word – late. Like someone was inconsiderate and just didn't show up when needed. Not that she was gone now, never to come back.

And although they never would have a full explanation, it seemed like DJ was heading to the border with Congo at the time she disappeared in January. And so this country held a sinister feeling for Lena. Even though she had agreed to come and start her communications work here, she was not comfortable. Little movements in her peripheral vision felt threatening somehow.

She reached over and made sure her mosquito net was tucked tight under all four corners of her mattress. She pulled the sheet around her shoulders, despite the night-time heat. She needed to protect herself, even though she wasn't sure from what.

# Four

## Bene

He makes his way east along the Seine as it curves towards the centre of the city. On the north side, he sees the edge of the Tuileries Garden. The Louvre will be up ahead. He wants to see the legendary glass pyramid, the contradiction between 21st-century glass and 18th-century stone palace. He read somewhere that people protested at the radical new building, and threated to throw cobblestones at the finished piece to see the glass shatter.

How could people get so upset over progress? Seems backward, wishing the future to be only in line with the past. What's the purpose of imagination, if we are only allowed to mimic what's already been done?

Gil thinks he's crazy for caring so much about cities and architecture. He thinks they will always change, never last. Gil is an ocean guy. He wants to study marine biology and always wants to live by, or preferably on the water, the fewer structures in the way the better. Bene's not like that. Sure, he loves to surf and that will always be his sport. The ocean is in his blood, but he doesn't see that as a contradiction to also wanting to build and explore on land.

He needs to find his way into the back alleys and the new experimental corners of these places. The famous sites that have been underfoot for thousands of years, shaped and pounded and shat on by people since the beginning of civilisation. He has to be there, to experience it first-hand. Paris now. Nairobi, next. Then where? Who knows? São Paolo? Tokyo? Here's hoping. He'll need to get that architecture scholarship though. No chance in hell without that.

It's something he's been arguing with Mum about, too much. She travelled the world when she was young but then managed to get stuck in Madeira. Her curiosity must have driven her once, but now there's just nothing. Something disappeared. She's left sitting in front of a broken desk, books wedged under the lame leg so that it doesn't wobble too badly. Pounding out her letters to prisoners of conscience every month, without fail. She hosts the local Amnesty International meetings: little ladies a hundred years old, with yellow teeth and smelling of mouldy paper. They are kind, he knows that. And they're doing their charity bit, which is better than remaining ignorant. But there's something about them that is stuck in that place, remembering life rather than seeking it out. It's holding everything back, holding him back. He needs to be out there, with people of his generation.

Mum has never stopped him; it's just that he's never had the chance before now. But she should know her family history better than anyone: they all travelled. Her mother and father left Portugal for London. DJ, then Mum worked in Angola, Sudan, Congo... Even with Aunt Magda, her first and most enduring love is with her sailing boats, and how they can take her away someplace else.

Mum has to remember that feeling – of wanting to be there, anywhere. It doesn't even matter where 'there' is. Just feeling the need to be on the move and living life.

No, she must have forgotten. She's buried herself in her homemade darkroom with nothing but her chemicals and abstract art and her work at the photography library. Now she insists on taking pictures of objects representing things, and patterns in nature, rather than going out to find the things themselves. He doesn't get it. Where did her exploring instinct go?

Maybe it's a man thing. She's a woman, and she has never stuck with a man very long. Her father died when she was twenty. She has no brothers. She's observed Bene growing up, but he was a boy then. She doesn't know what it means to be a man. He's going to have to do this last bit on his own.

He reaches the end of the Tuileries Garden and sees the tip of the Louvre Pyramid. It really is grand. The sun hits it full strength on the west side, rendering that triangle opaque. The other sides are transparent and he can see people descending the escalator into the chamber inside. What a feat of engineering. Whoever wanted to smash it was crazy.

He doesn't feel like being indoors. On a day like this, you are supposed to be celebrating the summer solstice. Stay above ground and breathe in the atmosphere, absorb the sunlight as if there is no tomorrow.

He sees a green labyrinth. He's not sure if he is supposed to wander through it or just admire it from the outside. Hell, he's a tourist. Isn't he supposed to mess up some rules? He walks through the paths but is disappointed. It's not a real maze, just an over-decorated hedge. No suspense there.

Out the other side, a group of people are clustered around another guitarist. This one has a small amp and is attempting the riff from 'Stairway to Heaven'. He is quite bad, but no one seems to judge him harshly. He's wearing a black bowler hat and a thin scarf wrapped twice around his neck, leaving a gap between the wool and the collar of his sleeveless t-shirt. A few people are watching and nodding to the rhythm of the music. But most are chatting or looking around, as if they are in someone's living room and expecting a cool kid to show up.

Bene puts his hands in his pockets, looks at his shoes, and walks on.

# Lena

### Bunia, Democratic Republic of Congo, July 2002

From the air, the rainforest looked like the storms had washed it into a dark green tangle. Lightning bolts flashed in the distance, and she wondered what the risk was for this small propeller plane. The pilot jerked the machine left and right to stay on course. The trees were only a short distance below. Were they supposed to be flying so low? It seemed as if the wings could almost touch the branches. She hoped it was only an optical illusion as she tightened her grip on the armrests.

She pretended she was used to these propeller planes, wearing her CWW staff shirt and holding her camera bag at her feet. But Congo felt so different than Angola. She had never seen a true rainforest before, and now she had a sense of how thick it was, with no chance of glimpsing the ground. In Angola it was dry and bleak, and you could see for miles in every direction when you were in the air. The challenge was trying to make sense of what lay buried under the soil – the legacy of landmines.

Landing in Bunia, she stepped onto a mud runway cleared in the forest. She was alarmed by a tank approaching at a fast clip, but then she realised it was painted light blue and emblazoned with a UN logo. It pulled up in front of the plane, perpendicular to the runway and blocking the way. It left deep tread marks in the mud, which sagged into a jagged pattern.

Out of the hatch of the tank came four soldiers in blue helmets and UN uniforms. They were tall Asian men with identical well-kept long black beards. Their laced high combat boots protected them from the mud as they stood to attention.

'Fucking peacekeepers,' the pilot muttered, shaking his head as he descended the plane's stairs. He marched up to them and started shouting. 'What the fuck! My runway!' He gestured wildly at the treads. 'What the hell are you doing?'

A UN officer was the last to come out of the tank. He was a light-skinned European, wore a beret, and had more stripes on his uniform than the others. He moved slowly, as if to emphasise his own importance. As he stepped towards the pilot he held up a hand to stop the obscenities.

'Please, *monsieur*, language,' he tutted in a French accent. 'We are not here to molest your runway. We are here to prevent smuggling.'

The pilot was not impressed by rank or gestures. 'For fuck's sake!' he said, ignoring the wince on the senior UN officer's face. The others remained expressionless. 'I'm bringing in relief workers, not militias.'

'I can see that,' the UN officer said. 'But we still must search your plane.' He signalled to the four soldiers to go inside and inspect, despite the pilot's objections. 'In case of stowaways, you understand,' the officer said.

He turned to Lena, and gave her a condescending smile. 'You are expected? With CWW?'

She nodded, and held out her passport towards him.

'Not to me, dear girl!' He waved it away as if administrative tasks were beneath him. 'Over there. Check in at immigration.'

Two more peacekeepers stood on either side of a desk, squatting in the open air at the side of the runway. The desk's fake veneer had peeled away from the plywood underneath, which had started to swell through the gaps with the humidity of the rainforest. A small Congolese man, hunched with layers of clothing and age, sat between the peacekeepers and pointed to a wilted sign that said *PAY VISA IÇI*.

Lena walked up to the desk. 'Visa?' she asked. 'We're still in Congo, aren't we? I haven't left the country.'

The man frowned as he reached for her passport. 'You are in Iturri, *madame*. Different administrative section,' he said. 'Twenty dollars US.'

She fumbled in her money belt and found the cash. The man confirmed with a nod and put a solid stamp down, taking up a whole page in the passport. Rain hit the stamp mark before he managed to close it, leaving a blurry ink drop to squash into the pages.

'No receipt,' he said.


Abbé Augustin had a kind face which got rounder when he smiled. His body, too, was round and his belly showed like a healthy melon underneath a custom-made shirt in rainbow colours celebrating Mother Teresa. A local priest working with the Catholic church's humanitarian mission, he managed the water projects for CWW across a wide range of territory. As part of this work, he and his small team organised peacebuilding activities for children.

'What exactly is peacebuilding?' Lena asked when she met him in the local CWW office. She didn't want to sound uneducated, but she found some of the jargon a bit vague.

'Oh, it can mean a lot of things,' he said. 'In this place, the war continues despite the peace talks in South Africa. The militias are aligned with different ethnic groups, and since the massacre in Nyankunde, people are really scared. The UN has reinforced the peacekeepers here, but they only control Bunia town.'

She was already composing photographs in her mind, how the landscape would overshadow the individuals, the dappled light coming through the shade of the dense canopy.

'For those of us who live or work outside of Bunia, though,' he continued, 'we have little protection.' He clasped his hands together in worried prayer. 'Although we pray to God.'

'You still go out to the villages in the bush?'

'That's where the projects are, so we have to try. But when the Ugandans withdrew their troops, they had funded lots of networks of militias. The Rwandese, too, have their networks. The Congolese government –' He noticed her disbelief. 'Yes, the DRC troops are part of the problem here as well. Everyone is contesting and manoeuvring for power and allegiance.'

'And the people are caught in the middle,' she said, looking down at her camera bag in her lap. It seemed so much more complicated than Angola, where there were two clear sides in an old-fashioned cold-war scenario. This seemed more like atoms spinning around and colliding in unpredictable patterns, creating damage.

'So if anyone tells you this is an ethnic war, you have to contradict them.' Abbé Augustin leant forward, looking directly into her eyes. 'People are terrified and getting massacred, yes. But it's all serving a purpose. Different purposes. Militias are making money off the natural resources here, and control by fear. Others – well, they need to pay their debt to the mercenaries they've brought in. Easiest way to do that is by attacking villages and looting, or taking gold or other minerals that can be smuggled out easily. It's outsiders using the conflict as economic opportunity, with no consequences for themselves.'

The Abbé sat back down. 'So... peacebuilding, it's fragile stuff. We are trying to build from the grassroots up, to address the fear that people have and make sure it is not aimed at their neighbours. The villagers are very frightened, and fear being attacked again. They're traumatised. We need to work slowly-slowly to build people's trust in our projects and in each other.

'CWW is a water charity. Everyone needs water. So, we bring people together with a shared plan for water for two villages with different groups of people. We facilitate their communications. We gently encourage them to work together, depend on each other. They start to look after each other. Women do the water collection together. Their kids can play together, without fear of reprisals. And if we're lucky, and there are no *force majeure* events, then maybe we make some progress towards peace.'

'Can I take some photos of the projects?' Lena asked. 'That's what Kojo wanted me to do.'

'Of course, we set out tomorrow. First, though, tonight we have a peace concert.'

The colours were muted and calm as Lena and Abbé Augustin entered the chapel for the peacebuilding project's concert. The singing had already started and didn't stop when they came into the one-room church. The children wore purple and yellow robes; the girls had red scarves in their hair. They seemed to be of all ages, with older ones leading from the front. The dancing was subtle, just swaying of the hips left and right. The clapping was steady but quiet, providing the percussion as sound filled the room. It was a sustained song, circling back on itself again and again. There was no pause. The group collectively had no need to stop for breath.

Abbé Augustin led her to a chair. She felt self-conscious in her photographer's vest, her khaki trousers. She should have worn some form of traditional women's clothing. They might think she lacked respect; she hoped that her professional demeanour would be acceptable to them. Soon, with any luck, they would forget about her and just let her slide into the background. Once they lost any self-consciousness, that's when the best photographs would surface.

To her right was a very old woman wearing Congolese traditional dress. She looked regal despite the cloth being thin and colourless. The woman nodded her head and moved her hands as if to clap, but there was no sound.

Abbé Augustin leaned over to whisper: 'These children are a mix of youth from opposing villages. They are getting to know each other and share time in these singing sessions. Sometimes it is difficult to convince the parents that it is safe to come, but today we have a good number.'

'Is it okay to take photographs?'

'Yes, I asked before and explained that you were with CWA's regional office. It's fine.'

She slipped off the chair and swung her camera around in front of her. She started clicking the shutter, trying to capture the combination of tired hope and ritual rhythm in front of her.

She went down on her knees to get a different view, thinking about how to frame the children from another angle. From below, they looked taller and more confident. She changed her shutter speed so she wouldn't need a flash. Aiming to capture the feeling and sense of movement, she let the motion of the children's limbs blur while their faces were caught in time.

The old woman fluttered her hand, gesturing for Lena to get up. She resisted, taking a few more photos, zooming in on the girls' feet in the dust. Some were barefoot, with cracked heels. Others had tattered shoes, plimsolls without laces or ballet flats that had seen no dance stage.

The old woman grunted and urged Lena to get up with more urgency in her gestures. This time she acquiesced. The old woman wagged a disapproving finger.

'No one goes on the floor,' Abbé Augustin told her later. 'Not voluntarily, anyway.'

She tried to explain that the photos would be more interesting from new angles. He just shook his head.

'It's just not how we do things,' he said. 'If you had lived through the traumas that we have, you would understand. There are things that you simply cannot do.'

# Five

## Bene

To the river, for a different scene. Bene finds the closest bridge and speeds up his walking. C'mon mate, blend in. He feels as if his face is exposed and again, he misses his favourite hat.

The bridge spans the water and gives him a feeling of space. He walks halfway across and rests forward on the railing. Leaning his face over the water, he feels a breeze from below and it calms him. It's not the ocean, but it's something.

A tourist boat surprises him as it emerges from under the bridge. The deck is full of people with their sunglasses protecting them from the late afternoon sun. Most are looking at the Louvre and the Tuileries, but one girl looks his way. She doesn't have sunglasses and shades her eyes with her hand. A guy's arm is wrapped around her shoulders. She doesn't smile as they glide past.

There must be millions of tiny padlocks on this bridge. What were people thinking? All different sizes – brass, silver, plastic. That one won't last, the one with the green plastic. It's already cracking. The graffiti of hearts and kisses seem to be like they are saying something about true love. How cheesy.

Still, it changes the way the bridge looks. Instead of the steady, proper Parisian architecture, you get this anarchy of teenagers declaring their love, like Romeo and Juliet. Defying convention, in tacky green plastic. He kind of likes it, despite himself. He takes out his camera, gets down on his knees, and shoots a few pictures from an angle that accentuates the length of the bridge, with that cracked lock in the foreground.

Mum did some things right. When she gave him a digital camera, it was one of the best things that ever happened to him. She prefers old-fashioned print film. But he needs digital; he has plans. He and Gil are going to set up an e-Zine they designed. Just need to get that web designing guy on board too, to make sure the coding goes to plan. Gil's no good at that. And Bene doesn't really like going into that level of detail on the programming side. He's the photo guy.

He descends the other side of the bridge onto the sandy path. He is nearly knocked over by a jogger who swerves around him and doesn't look back. On the wall holding up the embankment there are old posters and graffiti. One shows a guy with a lion's body, with words saying he's dreaming of a girl. Bene is drawn to it and takes some photos, not sure why. He likes it that Paris isn't immune to graffiti. Otherwise it would seem too clean, and he'd have to seek out interesting pictures elsewhere.

He never was into tagging himself. Funchal is such a small city that the police would jump all over a kid who got started with graffiti. You only do it if you want to get a reputation, make a name for yourself for that kind of thing. Here, in Paris, there's a whole different energy. Like there's a new generation of voices that are pushing to emerge from beneath the perfect exterior and old-fashioned architecture. You see it in the scraps of peeling posters and scribbles in spray paint that only half make sense. He struggles to understand the phrases and the humour. But it still speaks to him, and cheers him.

He crosses another bridge, intending to go back to the Louvre, but this one touches on the tip of an island that he feels like exploring. Funny, an island in the middle of a narrow river. It's not like there's a lot of expanse here. Walking the streets, he feels like laughing. These are Paris city streets, but in miniature. Everything is tiny and connected to somewhere else. You have the illusion of floating, with the river flowing by, but the stone bridges back to the banks make it clear the island's not going anywhere.

It's nothing like a real island. Go to Madeira, and you see a different kind of person. Someone who knows about water. And space. Islanders are probably all half-adrift in their minds. They like to think of themselves as free, light-hearted, untethered. But half the time they are hiding away somewhere, not ready to face the wider world.

He crosses another bridge, a little one to a second island. Who knew there would be so many little islands in the Seine? Might be tricky as a boat driver. He hopes those guys communicate or something to make sure thay don't get into trouble. They must do. If that's your job, day in day out, you must. You've got to have the right communications.

He stops in a small café. Everything here seems small, as if space is eye-wateringly expensive. He struggles through his order of a *café au lait* but just about makes himself understood. He sits down and looks back through recent images on his camera. He likes some of the graffiti and the street shots just now. There's something distinctively French about them, even the ones with just peeling paint and crumbling plaster.

He clicks through earlier photos. Some are self-portraits, made for the contributors page of the Zine, if they ever pull it off. He looks at his floppy twists – hair too afro to obey gravity, not afro enough to fully defy it. He frowns and clicks further. It's not good to look too closely at photos of yourself. Can get you focused a bit too inward and unhappy.

Mum's photo comes up, the time he surprised her coming out of the darkroom. She hadn't seen him as she opened the door to inspect a contact sheet, too impatient to let things dry properly first. She'd forgotten that her glasses were perched on top of her head as she squinted into the tray to make out the tiny details. He snapped the photo noticing the shadows creeping away from the corners of her eyes and her disapproving mouth. Then as she heard the shutter there were four or five more shots in a row of her looking surprised, then annoyed and waving him away. But she couldn't help cracking a smile in the end.

He wonders how she is doing in London. Hope Lucian is okay. She seemed really worried when she heard from the hospital about his cancer. Thought that only happened to older people. Lucian's not old, he's about the same age as Mum. But she said he never stopped smoking, even after everyone else they knew had kicked the habit. They were children together, always had a connection from the Stockwell estates where Mum grew up. Don't think they were ever together – 'Not in that way,' as Mum would say. Still, there's a loyalty to him that no one else can match. Maybe it's because Mum lost all her family young; she has no one else left from her past to hold onto.

It's fine, travelling by himself. He is ready for it, sure. But it still feels strange. They've always been together when travelling before. He's half-expecting to turn around and see Mum coming after him, waving the passport he left in a café or something. Or slowing him down, wanting to photograph a small detail on a leaf or a pebble with her old-fashioned camera. She wouldn't see the results until they got back home and she developed the negatives, but she wouldn't mind. She liked it better that way.

She's all about the details. Nothing beautiful is ever overlooked. As if she is terrified that if she doesn't document something precious, it will disappear and somehow be her fault.

He pays the bill and stands up to leave to resume his exploring. As he walks out of the door, he pats his passport in his back pocket. Still there.


'*Ça veut dire quoi, exactement?*'

Is she talking to him? Why's she asking him about what the graffiti means? He looks at her and thinks no, not someone like her. She is absolutely gorgeous. Curling black ringlets hide half her face and her neck is a graceful, perfect length. She has a slender silver nose-ring, no chain-link accessories needed. She drags on a cigarette with a smile, like it was a special treat designed only for her.

'Sorry?' he says.

'Oh, are you English?' She speaks with a strong French accent.

'No, no. But I speak it. Better than my French.'

'I see.' She seems disappointed. She turns back to the graffiti he was photographing, a design like Pandora's box but with so much coming out of it he can see why she said that, about not knowing what it means. Snakes rise out of a block, twisting and balancing on a kind of mosaic table top. Above, there are figures in silhouette dancing around. To the side, some of the figures jump off and sneak away for a cheeky embrace. Other things rise out of the box – guns and sparks and screams on faces and who knows what else. It doesn't seem to say one thing as a piece of graffiti. Seems like it wants to say a lot of things.

She has big silver sunglasses that she pulls down from their perch on her head and wiggles them in front of her eyes. They're like fighter pilot glasses, too big for her face. 'I don't see the point,' she says. She pronounces it like 'zuh point', which makes him smile.

'Why do you think there's a point?' he says.

'There's always a reason, *non*?'

'The reason might just be for someone's tag. The signature, you know. Staking out territory. Artistic territory.'

'Snaking out territory? That's funny.' She puts the reflective glasses back on top of her head, pushing the curls back. 'You're funny, you know?'

He looks away and takes a few more frames with his camera. 'There,' he says, clicking through the filters then showing her the screen. 'It looks cool in sepia.'

She looks at the rust-tinted frame. 'I see, like, old-fashioned. All the colour – gone.'

'Not all the colour, just selected colour.' He chooses a lo-fi theme. 'Or you can do it that way, everything looks denim.'

She nods. 'Like Levi's.'

'Or this way, high contrast.' He shows her the screen filled with fluorescent greens and yellows.

'Ew, I don't like it.' She pushes his camera away. 'I hate that kind of colour. Makes me think of medicine.'

'As a medicine it probably would taste terrible.'

She looks at him and her mouth shows her amusement. 'My name is Fatima.'

'Bene. Short for Benedito. You speak very good English, Fatima.'

She smiles. 'So do you.'

'I was raised that way. What's your excuse?'

'We learn it here in school, don't you know? And I lived for a summer in London.' She looks over his shoulder for a moment, and then back at him. 'Are you here for *la Fête de la Musique*?'

'I was hoping someone would tell me where it was.'

'It's all around you, my friend!' She gestures in big circles and he sees, across the square, that she's right. Music is all around. There are clusters of parties in every direction, people relaxing and looking up to the impromptu performers, expecting a personal show. He's come across these groups of musicians and fans on every corner. How did he not see it before?

'So if you are here looking for music,' she continues, 'tonight's your night!'

'So that's it? A night of music, everywhere in the city?'

'Until dawn. You'll love it.'

# Lena

### Bunia, DRC, July 2002

They hadn't warned her about the mud. She'd never seen anything like it before. So thick across a road that it was half-solid, half-liquid, and nearly always threatening to change the course of the vehicle without warning. The landscape was painted orange-brown with it. It washed up off the road and coated the bottoms of trees. It splashed onto the bushes and muddied all the paths. The rainy season came early this year, Abbé Augustin explained.

The driver was calm as he swung the wheel in large gestures, trying to gain traction. No one else in the car was too worried. It seemed like they saw this all the time. Lena was in the front passenger seat, referring back to Abbé Augustin for guidance. There also were two Congolese nuns with them, getting a ride out to the village of Djugu, where more CWW water projects were. One nun was very elderly and the other deferred to her with every posture and gesture.

'*Attention*!' the driver said as the Land Rover lurched sideways. Lena heard the engine rev as the wheels lost traction.

She held onto the handle above the window with one arm, the other pressing against the dash to protect against the rocking and sliding of the vehicle. She heard a slick sound of the car gliding on the mud. Then, through the change in vibrations in her wrists, there was some sense that treads had contact again and traction was regained.

Abbé Augustin chuckled from the rear seat.

Lena told her heart to stop being so frantic. She needed to get used to this, if she was going to photograph anything of any importance. She was going where journalists were afraid to go. There were so many stories that needed to be told. CWW wanted her to be strong and focused. Toughen up, girl.

The driver kept urging the car forward. Looking ahead, Lena tried to anticipate which part of the road was a better choice. The well-worn treaded lines, or the patches in between. The driver had a concentrated grace which did not show alarm. He was focused. Every move mattered.

They turned a switchback curve to go up a steep hill. The engine revved louder. The tyres carved into the ground. Lena leaned her weight forward instinctively, as if that might help the car go up. The road was still slick, but a bit rockier as it rose, which improved the traction. To their left, out of the driver's window, there was a wall of the orange-brown mud. This ledge of a road was cut out of the hillside. To their right, out of Lena's window, the height cut away and there was a striking view of villages and valleys, soaked in their dark-green rainforest colours. Lena's instinct was to keep gripping the dashboard, or else she would have opened up her camera bag and composed a photo. The contrast of the rain clouds rolling in, stratospheric stripes of greys and scowling dark shadow, would have made a stunning composition. But it stayed only in her mind, her camera bag remaining safe and closed at her feet.

The car lurched towards the edge and all the passengers gasped. Even Abbé Augustin, who was trying to keep people cheerful. This made the driver laugh, as he gently spun the steering back the other way, towards the safer wall-side of mud. The car caught traction again and continued its uphill progress. The nuns and Abbé Augustin teased each other in a local language Lena didn't understand. But the meaning was clear: don't worry, don't be foolish.

There was another switchback, so now she was on the wall-side of mud, the driver's side on the outer edge. This was not more comforting. It felt like the wall could simply shove the car off the edge, if it wanted to.

The driver did not change stance, still leaning forward and gently moving his hands as needed. Everyone stopped talking. Maybe they were praying quietly in the rear seats, she couldn't tell. Maybe she should have been praying too.

Suddenly the car was slipping again. It glided in slow motion, perpendicular to the road. No tyre nor steering wheel could control that. Just the momentum of the car and the pull of gravity, moving towards the cliff-edge.

Lena instantly pictured them trapped in a metal box as it rolled off the ledge and crashed into the valley below.

'*Mon Dieu*,' said Abbé Augustin. The nuns whispered prayers and crossed themselves.

On instinct, Lena clicked her seatbelt and tugged it off, opened her door and jumped out. She landed between the car and the wall of mud. Her feet on the ground felt solid, much better than the horrible feeling of the car shifting on muddy layers.

The car was still gliding slowly towards the edge, but now she was outside the vehicle she could see that there was some ground before the drop. Not much, perhaps a foot and a half, but they were not quite on the precipice.

The driver took the car into the lowest gear and tried for traction again. This time the treads found something solid enough to grasp. The car lurched closer to the wall, nearly catching Lena then passing ahead.

Without a word to the others, she watched the car slowly make its way up the switchbacks. The passenger side door was slightly ajar, the seatbelt dangling. The car was progressing faster than her walking, but only just.

She followed in its wake. She felt embarrassed, like a child after a ridiculous outburst.

The rain was a soft mist on her face. She wished Kojo was there with her. So much of this was new; it was hard to tell what was really dangerous and what was normal in these circumstances. But would he have known any better? He had much more experience than her, sure. But Congo was a new place for him as well. It seemed more unfathomable than ever.

At the top of the hill, the car waited for her to finish the climb. The engine turned over calmly in neutral, like this was all a normal workday.

She climbed back into the passenger seat. 'Sorry,' she said. She felt bad that the driver might think she didn't trust him. 'I have faith in you,' she said to him. 'I just don't trust the mud.'

The driver smiled and said nothing, as he shifted into gear to drive on.

'I'm glad you jumped out,' Abbé Augustin said.

'You are?'

'Yes, I would have too, you know. I was very frightened. I lost a dear friend that way, going over a cliff on a muddy route in the rain. Lovely woman.'

'I'm so sorry...'

'But these two ladies,' he chuckled, gesturing to his fellow passengers to his left and right, 'they were blocking my exit.'

'Well, it's all fine now,' Lena said, trying to draw a line under it. Now that the car was on higher ground, and away from the cliff's edge, she felt like she had to re-establish her credentials. She took out her digital camera and started shooting the storm clouds coming over the valley.

She thought about that friend of Abbé Augustin's who went off the cliff. Wonder how often he thought of her... and if you ever can really forget a trauma you have heard about, but not lived through.

# Six

## Bene

He likes walking just a bit behind her, watching her curls bounce as she walks. Fatima changes direction, taking him across the river and into some smaller streets. She is wearing a loose shirt that goes past her waist, over skinny jeans. The fabric of the shirt is sheer enough for his eye to make out her curves underneath, her hips shifting left and right with her strides. She is confident and doesn't look back to check if he's looking.

'As you're an artist,' she says, 'you should see the *Centre Pompidou*.'

He tells her about his sculptures, and how he likes the industrial look. His love for museums and old-fashioned stuff, twisting the old into something new. He has told her too much already. Can't stop talking. He must seem like a blathering idiot. He stops when he sees a photo he wants to take – of more graffiti.

'That one...' she says. 'The band broke up after the lead singer overdosed. Then this graffiti went up all over Paris with this stencil of the guy's face with a mic. I think it was from his last concert.' She traces her hand over the shape of the singer's profile. 'It's so sad.'

She stops by a line of ripped posters of gigs. They are so old that graffiti is both below them and across them, making it into a wide mess of colour. 'Do you like abstract pictures?' she asks.

He takes close-up photos of the graffiti, the layers of weathered paper striped with paint and last year's rain. Then he steps back to get her in some of the shots as well. She puts back on her aviation glasses. She purses her lips and puts her hands on her hips. He has to laugh – she has so much personality, the photos won't do her justice. It could be a great series, like a stop-motion film. *Fatima in the City,* he'd call it.

'Look out!' she shouts, and pulls him towards her onto the pavement. He falls and hits his knee hard as a motorcycle zooms past, too close. His camera swings and smashes against his wrist.

'*Cretin!*' she yells at the driver, who ignores her as he turns a corner.

'Are you okay?' She kneels down and takes off the glasses, looking anxious. 'He almost hit you!'

'I'm alright,' Bene says, rubbing his knee and shaking out his wrist. He inspects his camera, and is relieved to find it is still working.

She smiles wide. 'I'm so glad. I would hate for you to be killed on your first night in Paris!' She kisses him on the cheek, smelling of vanilla and something spicier. Then she moves back in front of the graffiti.

He pretends the kiss doesn't mean anything. 'That's okay,' he says. 'I'm done with that shot.'

'Well, if you say so.' She takes him by the hand, the one not smarting from being smacked by the camera. 'Pompidou is just around the corner.'

She leads him past small cafés, bakeries, stores catering to tourists. They pass an old umbrella shop, all the colours in the window bleached by the sun. It sells the ones with those old-fashioned handles with the heads of snakes and eagles and things. The place looks so dusty he can't imagine anyone ever going inside. He takes a few photos of the animal-handles, then they walk on.

They see a hat store. It's not like the umbrella shop. It's caught up with the 21st century, selling all the latest knitted ones that skaters wear and the baseball styles for the American tourists. Some tacky magnets and things, Eiffel Tower keyrings, all for a few euros.

'Look at this place,' he says.

She looks at him strangely.

'I want a hat,' he pulls her inside.

'What for?' she asks.

'I left one at home, this brimmed hat I liked.' He really wants that hat back, so badly he would have paid fifty euros for it. The kind that shields you from the rain or the sun. You could wear it to keep the spotlights out of your eyes so you could concentrate when you got up in front of a crowd of thousands to play jazz on the world stage, your fans going wild. He tries to get Fatima to translate what he's looking for.

'*Pas la saison,*' says the sales clerk, and Fatima shakes her head in agreement. It wasn't the season for it, of course. A felted wool hat would sound ridiculous if you didn't think of it the right way, like the guy on stage. But how could they not see that it's not a winter thing, but a year-round master hat?

'No problem,' Bene says, trying not to show his disappointment.


The art museum is as gorgeous as she said. Industrial pipes climb up the building, as if the outside finish is in retreat and the steel tubing is rising up in dominance. They conquer everything and turn your expectations inside out. He likes the colours, and the escalator running up the outside. Never seen anything like it.

He takes loads of photos from far away and zooming close. He'll have a lot of fun playing with the colours and contrast later; now he just wants to catch it from every angle.

She sits on the pavement. It slopes downwards in a hill but it's also a play area for kids and students. He wanders to take photographs, and feels her eyes following him. But when he looks back, she is texting on her phone.

A street artist draws a scene for the tourists of a very large map with continents and flags. You're supposed to put your coins on the map where you're from. Or maybe where you're going, if you're just passing through. Indecisive people can just toss the coin into a metal bowl placed where Paris would be on the map. Coins make a *chi-chang* sound as they land in the bowl. One guy misses and the coin rolls away, a kid chasing after it. The artist raises his head to watch, then nods as the boy puts it in the collection where it was intended.

Bene looks at the map, considers his options. He decides to place his coin on top of Kenya, where he's heading. Makes as much sense as anywhere, really.

There is a children's entertainer, painted face and all, surrounded by kids. He has this rope strip thing so he can make a line of large bubbles out of a solution in a bucket at his feet. The kids squeal and jump, trying to pop the bubbles even before they leave the rope formation.

'This is great, so great,' Bene says, sitting down beside her on the slope. He wishes he had more sophisticated words to say what he feels.

A woman sings a mournful tune in one corner of the courtyard. A man stands behind her, sitting on a stool with one foot higher than the other, playing a guitar, flamenco-style. She has an audience circled around her; they are entranced. Eyes all on her, there is none of the casual chatting on the sidelines.

'That's Fado,' he tells Fatima.

'No, it's Arabic,' she says.

'It's a Fado tune, I know it!'

'It's a traditional North African song. Maybe you Portuguese stole it.' She gives him a look like he's done something naughty. 'Listen.' She hums along with the woman, then adds words when it comes to a chorus. He can't follow the meaning but doesn't want it to stop.

'What's it mean?'

'Oh, you know. Love, broken hearts, that sort of thing.'

'No happy ending?'

'It doesn't really have an ending. It circles in on itself as long as the audience wants to listen.'

They watch in silence. The woman sings with her eyes closed, standing nearly motionless except for her lips. Her jawbone seems to be working hard, holding tight around the mournful notes. Her face is lined with tension, as if she is reliving a pain from long ago.

Somehow, the audience knows when it is about to end, and start to applaud as she holds a final note. The guitarist strums wildly like this is his last chance for fame. Then the woman's posture relaxes, her eyes open and her face rises into a smile that almost looks like she doesn't know who was just making all that sadness out loud. She places her hand on her heart and takes a bow.

'The night is still young,' Fatima says as the crowd starts to get up and move on. 'Do you want to see some more music?'

He nods. He'd do anything for this girl. Got to make sure he doesn't fall in over his head. He needs something, for courage. 'How about a drink first?' he says.

She looks at him. 'How old are you?'

'Eighteen,' he lies. 'Nineteen very soon.'

'I know a place,' she says.

# Lena

### Goma, DRC, July 2002

After flying down south again, Lena sat on her bed in the guesthouse in Goma with her laptop on her knees, her mosquito net draped above. She wanted to type up quick notes about the photos before the details escaped her. The impressions of the short trip to Bunia – the cars in the mud, the quiet determination of Abbé Augustin and the nuns, the peace chorale, the community water projects, the UN peacekeepers who seemed both under-staffed and inadequately equipped – how to turn these into a short report from the field? She'd never done this before, and tried to think the best way through.

The people, she convinced herself. Capture the stories about the people, and the projects and politics will come to matter because of the impact on people. She pounded out her thoughts on the laptop without much editing, hoping her language was taking the shape of an aid worker: professional, factual, descriptive, to the point.

She took a break for dinner. The guesthouse had a bar at the back, hanging with vines of bougainvillea, overlooking Lake Kivu. Gisenyi, a town in Rwanda, was just across the water. Points of light shimmered from lake-houses and docks. As the sun dropped, Rwanda got dark first, with night approaching from the east. A crescent moon perched above low mountains around the lake.

Earlier, the bar had a relaxed feeling, with soft music playing. People spoke quietly over beers, cold from the generator-powered fridge. She had been looking forward to hearing the band play, with the breeze from the lake cutting away the heat of the day.

Now, however, the place was packed, and the air was tense. Most of the crowd were young men, and many of them were in the military. They stood tall and confident, in clean pressed uniforms, with their shoulders back and berets on at an exact tilt. There was little banter or laughter. Guns were everywhere: some were resting on the bar, others were dangling off a strap, like a camera. Others were held ready, the soldier's finger in position on the trigger.

She went up to the bar for a menu, then paused a moment. Who could she trust here? She caught a glimpse of the bartender and waited until he came near so she could ask him what was going on.

He looked around to see who was within listening distance before whispering: 'It's one of the VPs. From Kinshasa. He's decided to stay here for the night. With entourage.'

'One of the vice presidents? How many are there?'

He looked at her as if she really shouldn't have asked. 'Four, don't you know? And they are all competing for power. They show off their wealth in soldiers. He's taken over most of the rooms. If I were you, I'd find another place to stay.'

She looked around at all the armed men, trying not to show her alarm. She was by herself with no contingency plan, nowhere else to go. She took her chicken and rice to her room to eat, hoping to become invisible.

There was an old chest of drawers in the room. Made of dark lacquered wood, it was nearly as tall as she was. She leaned with all her weight and pushed it towards the door: her own personal barricade. If anyone tried to force their way in, at least there would be some resistance. There was a dark patch on the wall where the chest of drawers had been. She hoped no one had heard the screech of wood dragging on the floor. She didn't want to raise any suspicion.

What was she doing here, a woman travelling alone, no experience in Congo, no background in this kind of thing? She could be anywhere. She should be anywhere else.

She looked out of the window, the colour of the sky darkening as the sun fell out of sight behind the hills. Lake Kivu was black and calm. According to the locals, underneath the depths were balls of sulphuric gas that could rise in a moment, although they seldom did. Perhaps life was precarious everywhere, but here it felt even more so.

She fell asleep in her clothes, sitting on the floor with her back against the chest of drawers.

She heard a high alarmed ringing. She looked at her phone, but it wasn't her ringtone. It said 2:08 am.

Many ringtones went off all at the same time. Some were urgent, piercing rings, others were less shrill. Some were a few recognisable notes from pop songs – Ricky Martin, Britney Spears, others she couldn't name. They were all ringing at once, clashing and building into an uncontrolled racket.

Then there were footsteps — urgent, running footsteps, responding to commands. There was a muddle of male voices, some shouting, others in quiet agreement. The words were muffled through the walls but it seemed like some orders were being given, changes were happening at a pace. There were knocks on doors, sounds so close they made her jump. Doors opening, more orders drilled into someone. Shutting doors, more footsteps. More ringtones. More knocking.

Each time she heard a hand turn a doorknob she started. She prayed it wasn't her door. Each time, miraculously, hers was overlooked.

She awoke to the sound of birdsong over the lake. From her position on the floor she could see the sky out of the window – seemed to be just mist and a hint of the other shore in the distance. No signs of the commotion of the night.

Her neck was stiff from sleeping sitting up, and she rolled her shoulders back. Her hand tingled where she had been leaning on it. She shook both hands at the wrists as she stood up and tried to decide what to do. Had she imagined all the ringtones and footsteps?

She quickly packed up her clothes, notes, laptop and cameras. They fit into two small bags. With effort, she moved the chest of drawers back to its place. It was much heavier than she remembered.

She opened the door. In the hallway the smell of cigarettes hovered like a shadow and stubs littered the floor. Footprints muddied the linoleum, concentrated on the doorway next to her own. Maybe that was where the vice president had been staying.

Downstairs at the bar, there was almost no one, and not a machine gun in sight, thank God. The place was trampled and abandoned-looking. She saw the bar owner, nursing a morning cup. He gestured for her to help herself to the instant coffee.

'What happened?' she asked, spinning a spoon through Nescafé streaked with powdered milk.

His eyes were bloodshot, and he was wearing the same shirt as last night. It was missing the top two buttons and exposed a smooth chest. 'The VP got a call in the middle of the night. The rebels took Goma airport for a time and his personal helicopter was set on fire. The rebels have cleared out now, but it showed that Goma is not safe under the government.' He blew some air out in a rush. 'It's a bloody nose to him and to Kinshasa. He was really pissed about it. Didn't pay his bill, the bastard.'

He looked up at her, as if he hadn't thought about her until that moment. 'What are you still doing here? Most of the internationals cleared out last night.'

'I was just in my room.'

'Usually you people have your security protocols to follow, no?'

She looked at her mobile phone. It didn't always have reception, but it did now. Someone should have contacted her, shouldn't they?

She had a quick breakfast and paid her bill. If all the other internationals had already left, did that make her a potential target? Ill informed, and left behind?

She walked out to the veranda, where the view of Lake Kivu was calm. She kept thinking about the ringtones for some reason, and the hands on the doorknob of the room next to her own. The mist was lifting off the surface of the water to reveal a layer with no hint of disturbance.

She rang Kojo's number. Several rings went by before he picked up.

'Morning,' he said, voice rumbling as if he hadn't yet spoken to anyone today.

The story came out in a rush – about the armed men in the hotel, the noises in the night, the chest of drawers, the reports of the rebels at the airport. Kojo listened carefully and repeated details back to her in summary, just to ensure that he understood.

'Damnit, I was hoping you could get out of Congo without an incident. Your first mission as a regional rep, and this happens. Security should have rung you or left a message with the hotel. Stand by, I'll ring you back. I'll radio Bukavu and Kigali, to see if they know anything more.'

She hung up the phone. She had no way of calibrating her own sense of danger to the actual situation. She couldn't go back into the hotel room and barricade herself in forever. She wondered what might have happened if she hadn't had a strong set of drawers there and someone had tried to force their way into her room. She wouldn't have had any real defence.

If the rebels took the airport, what other way was there to get home? And where was home, anyway? When she thought of joining Kojo, she thought of the villa they'd shared in Angola. But she was supposed to go to Nairobi after this, a place she'd never been.

The smell of last night's chicken barbecue wafted up from the charred half-barrels below. She wondered what had been decided at yesterday's party.

The mist was burning away. She could see more of the lake now. It was surrounded by low mountains, formed in layers descending towards the water. She would have loved to swim, but she knew that wasn't allowed. Two elegant crested cranes skimmed and then landed on the water. Were they the type to mate for life, or just a season?

Kojo rang back. 'With the airport attack, the security team assess that the risks are too high for you to stay on in Goma. And your mission was nearly concluded anyway. You know the main road in town? I think...' She heard the rustling of a map on the other end. 'That main road – Kigali Road... you need to walk that to the border, then go to Gisenyi, the first town on the Rwanda side. There you can take transport to Kigali.'

'You want me to walk to Rwanda?'

'It's not far. Do you have your medical kit?'

'Yep. And my passport and my letter from CWW with my *laissez-passer*.' She hadn't known why she needed a special letter that just asked for a generic permission to pass, but this seemed to be the right occasion.

'Great. Keep that on your person at all times. Don't let go of that, or your passport if you can help it.'

'When should I go?'

'Now. Call me as soon as you cross the border.'

# Seven

## Bene

Fatima takes him to a tiny place, down some stairs with candles dripping wax into mismatched crockery lining the way. The walls are painted black, and a purple-tinged blacklight makes anything white stand out. There's a stripe on her bag, hanging on her shoulder; it is now fluorescent purple-white. Her teeth too, when she smiles back at him, look alien. He's relieved when her mouth closes back over them again. Her lips are a dark shade in this atmosphere.

It might be a student bar. There are posters up for gigs and protests, it seems. He can't read all the words, but he can make out that some of the events are connected to the student union.

'This your kind of place?' he asks, as she ushers him to sit at a round table about as big as a dinner plate. There is only enough space for a tiny candle and her elbows. In response to a small gesture from Fatima, a waiter brings a carafe of what might be wine, although the lighting is so weird it could be anything. He laughs a bit to himself.

'What's so funny?' she asks. She leans forwards, chin in hands, on that tiny little table that can barely support anything.

'Nothing, no...' He tries to think of something brilliant to say, but it escapes him. 'Is this your uni?'

'Uni? *C'est quoi*?'

'University?'

'Ah, yes. *Ponts* is my university. It's very well known – haven't you heard of it? *L'École des Ponts ParisTech*. Very prestigious, I think you would say. My father was very proud of me to get in. You see, I'm the first of my family to seek a degree. I'm training to be an engineer-architect.'

'You – an architect! That's amazing!'

'Why, you think I can't do it?'

'No, that's not what I meant, it's just... you don't look like... what I mean is that... I really want to be an architect. I'm trying to get a scholarship.'

'Well, they do let women do it too, you know.' She looks annoyed. He's said the wrong thing, disappointed her by being stupid.

'I didn't mean that,' he said. 'You know I didn't. It's so cool.'

'You think so? My friends don't think so. It's a lot of hard work and I miss out on everything.'

'Everything? Can't be true. You're here with me, aren't you?'

She nods and looks away. He wonders why she is free and alone on the night when everyone else in Paris is in the streets celebrating with friends.

'You're going to build great things, you know,' he says.

She looks up at him, hopeful, but then her eyes change as if she is not sure if she can believe him. 'Why do you say that?'

'I can feel it. You're destined for greatness. Huge skyscrapers, monuments, they will all bow down to you.' He's being silly now, anything to bring that smile back to her face.

'What is that, *destined*?'

'When something is meant to be.'

'Like you meeting me, in front of the graffiti?'

'Maybe. We'll have to see how the night ends up.'

'Funny boy.' She lifts the carafe and pours the drink. The glasses are small, like they were made for milk, not wine. They might be jam jars. He lifts his glass up and smells deep tones of red berries, although in that strange lighting it looks like melted stone. He takes a sip. It is smooth and a little bit acidy, not at all sweet like the cheap drinks he and Gil managed to get hold of from the corner shop behind school. But he's never sat at a bar like this, with a girl he wants to impress. He pretends like he does this kind of thing every night.

'So where are these friends,' he says. 'I'd like to meet them to tell them how cool it is to be an architect.'

'You want to meet them? I don't know if they are your type.'

'Type, what type? I'm an open-minded person. Although if they want to speak French to me, I go slow.'

'Arabic, more likely.'

'Oh, I'm no good then. We'll have to resort to using our hands in sign language or something.'

She snakes her arm between the glasses and rests her hand on top of his. 'Or something.'

# Lena

### Goma, DRC, July 2002

It was still cool for the morning, but Lena knew it would heat up soon. The soles of her shoes creaked as they marked the dirt road not yet fully dry from the rainy season. She walked in the direction of the border and caught views of the lake through gaps in the trees. The mist was gone now, leaving the surface unprotected. She thought about the poisonous gases stored underneath, wondering what would make them rise.

There were few sounds, and she saw no other European faces. Not many people were about at all. She didn't want to stand out, but there was nothing she could do about that. A pick-up truck rolled past her without slowing, then weaved around the potholes filled with muddy rainwater that failed to evaporate. Six men sat in the back of the pickup. Their clothes were of the same cloth, a dust-stained faded uniform. They looked at her but did not smile.

Roadsides that yesterday had women selling vegetables were now abandoned. The only signs of life were residual: a broken plastic sandal in a roadside ditch; burnt corn-cobs discarded next to a charred barbecue pit. The silence was eerie. Shacks set back from the road were quiet and closed. She had the feeling that people were watching her through shaded windows or hidden behind doors.

She reached the border post after walking for about twenty minutes, as Kojo said she would. It was guarded by Congolese soldiers in grey and tattered uniforms. They took little interest as she approached. There was a chain stretched across the road so no vehicles could cross. One man in a folding chair sat with his hand on the latch where the chain met a wooden stake. He chewed on a toothpick and refused to meet her eyes. She walked around the barrier and followed a footpath towards a small shack.

Inside there was a woman in the same army uniform, but hers was cleaner and pressed. She had a beret and badges of rank. She sat on a plastic chair but had no desk. An old green metal box was perched on her lap. There were no more seats. On the floor sat a woman in a Congolese wrapped dress, the material faded and worn. Two babies, twins perhaps, were tied to each side with fabric that looked old and tired. The ties had lost their tension and the babies flopped to either side. One was curled with eyes closed, asleep or just shutting out the stimuli. The other looked at Lena as she walked in, chewing on the side of its small fist. The woman looked straight ahead, muttering small worried sounds that only she could understand.

The officer tapped on her metal box and demanded to see Lena's passport and papers. She studied the photo in the British passport for a moment. She unfolded the *laissez-passer* note and ran a finger along the lines of type. She grunted when she matched the names on the note and the passport.

'Magdalena Gloria Rodrigues,' she read out loud. She held onto the letter a bit longer, then rummaged in her box for a wooden stamp. Looking up, she said, 'Twenty dollars, US.'

Lena nodded and handed over a wilted bill.

The officer inspected it, frowned at a small tear but tucked it into a brown paper envelope hidden under her belt. She put a firm stamp into the passport, on the *laissez-passer,* and on a third small slip of paper. She wrote a tight squiggle of a signature, then closed the box with a bang that startled the babies, and they began to cry. The mother gently bounced the children without getting up or turning her gaze from the open door that looked to the trees and border soldiers outside.

The officer made it clear that she was done with Lena, and pointed her in the direction of Rwanda. There was a walk of about a hundred metres of dirt road before another barrier. For that time, Lena was in no man's land. She wondered what happened if someone was attacked in the space between two countries. Whose protection would you have? Maybe you're only a liability to yourself. Or perhaps prey to anyone.

She looked behind her. The man with the toothpick was still there, guarding the road from Goma. Not a soul on the Congolese side took any interest in her at all. She could have disappeared last night, or any night, and no one here would have noticed.

Ahead of her, half a dozen soldiers in fresh green uniforms and sunglasses stood alert in front of a metal guardrail. Their machine guns were held with both hands, ready to fire. Behind them the road was tarmacked, and there was a retractable line of metal spikes threatening to puncture any tyre, if someone tried to proceed without permission. The soldiers examined her as she approached. She felt exposed and shabby, with her khakis and her two backpacks slung across her shoulders.

'*Bonjour*,' she said to the one standing closest to her path. He didn't respond but cocked his head sideways to indicate the way for pedestrians. The immigration building was made of concrete blocks with solar panelling on the corrugated iron roofing.

Inside there were about a dozen empty chairs. A fan twisted above, making Lena feel the cold of her sweat from carrying the bags. A small man with a thin face sat behind thickened glass. He was looking into the screen of a computer, which lit his face with a green glare.

Through a crescent-shaped hole she passed her passport and papers. With a slight nod, he skimmed the documents and tapped the information into his database.

'Fifty dollars please,' he said. She obliged, realising that her money was getting low. A printer behind him came alive and scrolled out a small adhesive square that he pressed into her passport. She was relieved when she held it in her hands again.

'Welcome to Rwanda,' he said.

# Eight

## Bene

They get off the Metro at La Muette. Fatima says she knows people having a party. University people. *Ponts* people. Having their own *Fête de la Musique*. Bene would rather stay outside, wander the streets all night, but she seems keen to go. He swallows hard and tucks in his white t-shirt – maybe it won't look so cheap if the place has low lighting.

Why is she hanging out with him? He doesn't get it. A beautiful woman like her, in a university, friends all around the city… what does she need a kid like him for?

She pulls him into a liquor shop, asks him what he likes. He shrugs and tells her to get whatever. While she makes her choice, he studies the labels of the bottles. Some are dusty as if they haven't been touched in years. Others are clean, colourful and bright, as if trying to draw in new customers, like attracting children to sparkling new playthings.

She pays for a bottle, and leaves in a sudden rush. Holding his hand, she hurries through the narrow streets and then stops in front of huge wooden gates. They are shellacked and shiny, as if the same brown colour has been applied for centuries without a hint of change. She types in a code on the security keypad, and a smaller door opens up, leaving the bigger doors standing in place. He has to duck his head to get through.

'You're tall, for a young kid,' she says.

'That door is short, for something, like, a hundred years old.'

'More like two hundred,' she says.

'Is it your flat?'

'No, I've just been here a lot.'

'Your friend's place?'

'No. My ex.'

He pulls the straps a bit tighter down on his backpack. He wishes he was wearing a better shirt, something more sophisticated. What if her ex is a complete prat? Or what if she wants to get back together with this guy, and leaves him stranded? What a mess of an evening that would be.

He should be back at the hostel. Is there a curfew for getting back? He forgot to check; that was stupid. Last thing he needs is to be locked out all night on the streets of a city where he doesn't belong. He pulls the key out of his pocket. On the key fob it states that doors are locked at midnight. His watch shows 21:30. Three hours almost. Plenty of time. Sun hasn't even set yet.

She presses a button for the lift. It is a tiny one that only just fits into the elbow of the curved banister of the old-fashioned wooden staircase. 'Put that away,' she said, pointing to the key fob. Then she turns to look at him. She seems to think he passes some test, nods in approval. The lift comes and it is the smallest he's ever seen. Two people barely fit. If they had more wine, they would probably go past the weight limit. She puts her face very close to his, her lips to his ear.

'Look,' she whispers, 'I'm sorry I didn't tell you before. This is Gabriel's place. I promised him I'd stop by. But we don't have to stay long. I said I was busy tonight, with someone I knew from a long time ago. So, if you could just go with it, that would be fantastic. Just a few minutes here and then we'll disappear. I'll take you to a party with some really fun people. The people here, well...' They get out of the lift on the third floor. She presses the buzzer for a flat in the middle of the length of hallway. 'They can be a bit pretend.'

'Pretend? They're not real?'

'Kind of. You know, fake.'

He nods. He's not looking forward to this party.

'One last thing. Can you say you're older? And visiting from Portugal or something? Tell me a name of a university there.'

'*Universidade da Madeira.*'

'Perfect. You are a second-year student there. You'll fit right in with all the other people pretending to be someone they're not.'

The door opens and it's a blonde woman, wearing a black turtleneck as if she doesn't care that it is June. Fatima gives her a kiss on both cheeks and leans closer to say something. The woman gives her a half-smile, and looks at Bene. Her eyes go up to his twists and down to his clothes. She leans to give an air kiss near each cheek like it is a duty, not a pleasure. She smells like the dusty perfume of an old auntie.

It's a funny kind of party. They pass a small kitchen littered with cups and empty bottles of hard liquor and wine. The room off the hallway is large, very white and very empty. The music is quite loud, from a sound system, not a musician. It plays to the vacant room.

Most of the people are out on the balcony. Not too many though – he can see maybe eight or nine through the wide glass doors. Bene watches Fatima from behind as she moves to the balcony door. She looks back at him, and signals that she'll just be a minute. Then she is gone.

He sits down with a flop onto a beige sofa that looks like someone dry-cleaned it yesterday. Whoever lives here must have money. He wonders if it's really Gabriel's place, or his parents'. A place like this in a city like Paris, they must be loaded. There are abstract paintings, all variations of the tan colour. A vinyl collection is lined up, black and straight in an otherwise beige-tinted world. He gets up and looks at some of the titles. Many he doesn't recognise – seems like a lot of old French men with long hair. No one outside of France would've heard of any of them. But the cover photos on the albums – of live concerts, fans throwing their arms up and reaching for the singer – make it seem like they are treated like the messiah or something.

He looks again for Fatima, seeing if he can make out her silhouette amongst the others on the balcony. He thinks that's her, the woman with the curls making her way towards the left. There is a view of the Eiffel Tower, you can see it through the gaps in the buildings. It sparkles, lasting for about a minute, and then goes back to steady light.

After a little while, two girls stumble into the room from the balcony, giggling as they cling to each other. One looks up and sees him. '*Pardon,*' she says, trying to be polite. Then she turns back to her girlfriend, and they fall onto another couch across the room. They are excited and secretive at the same time. The one who didn't acknowledge him is rummaging in her handbag. When she finds what she is looking for, she clears a little space on her lap while shielding some objects from view. It is only when the other takes out her wallet and starts to roll a twenty-euro note that it clicks what's happening. He looks away.

How many bills get used like that? The snot laced with cocaine that must be circulating in this city, any city, from parties like this.

He stands up. This isn't his kind of scene. Doesn't make any difference to the snorters; they are in their own little world. He needs to tell Fatima that he has to get out of here.

He goes to the balcony and sees that it is very narrow. You can only pass by people if they lean back and hold their breath. With apologies he squeezes past several people with their wine glasses. They don't object, but they don't rush to move either. Most of them are focused on a singer below in the square.

The singer has a circle of people cheering and a friend behind him on a keyboard. He shouts out with gusto in English, 'Sing us a song, you're the piano man...' With the French accent it sounds like he's begging someone, anyone, to sing. It's working: lots of people sing along in a mixture of drunk voices. He's still the obvious lead, though. Anyone who takes to the mic like that needs to have some guts. The piano guy behind him is pretty good. He has some skill and is really on fire. The singer, well... take it or leave it, really.

Fatima is towards the end of the balcony, talking to a guy much taller than she is. He is more than two metres tall, a giant or something. How does he get through that door at the entrance? Must bend nearly double. It's funny how rich people live.

Bene tries to say something, but she interrupts with, 'There you are!' She introduces him to Gabriel as her *copain*. Gabriel is good looking, you have to say that. He has huge eyes and a face that women probably think is very handsome. His hair is dark and falls over one eye. His clothes look expensive and like someone pressed them just before the party started. He says a few things to Bene in French, and then tries Spanish. Turns out his mum is Spanish, and his dad is someone high up in the French government. Bene can understand Spanish okay, but feels too tongue-tied to reply. Monosyllabic answers come out as he tries to remember what role Fatima wanted him to play.

Fatima slips her hand into his. In English, she says, 'I'm just so lucky Bene has a break from his uni. You know, we don't see each other often enough.'

Gabriel seems to understand English but replies in French, something fast and meant only for Fatima.

She doesn't let go of Bene's hand, and for that he's grateful. But he still wants to get going.

'Um...' he improvises. 'We do need to get going. You know, for that thing?' He gestures out the window to some vague destination. 'That thing you talked about?'

'Of course,' she says. 'I lost track of time.'

'No problem at all. Unless you want to stay longer?'

'Let's get moving.' She drops Bene's hand to stand on tiptoe to hold Gabriel's shoulders for a moment. She moves to kiss him once on each cheek. He holds her at the waist, for a moment – too long – and then lets go.

They squeeze past the wine drinkers again to get to the doorway. Just before going inside she points to the Eiffel Tower. 'Look!' They stop shuffling and watch the sparkle effect. 'They do it every hour during *la fête,*' she says. 'It adds to the atmosphere. Makes you feel like the whole city is singing.'

He nods, but his mind is on something else. These slim balconies. How many people think about jumping off them? How many actually do it? It would be so easy. Nothing to stop you, really. Just your own restraint.

He doesn't know why his mind goes to a morbid view of things. Can't help it.

'Do you ever think about, you know,' he motions with his head down below. 'Taking the plunge? Leaving it all behind?'

'No, do you?'

'My mum would never forgive the world if that happened.'

'I know what you mean. My parents too.'

'No, it's because she has absolutely no one else. No husband, no other kids. Just an old auntie who we live with, but really, I'm all she's got.'

'That's a lot of guilt to carry.'

'Guilt? Never thought of it that way. It's just the way we are. She's responsible for me growing up, so I'm responsible to her.'

She laces her fingers between his and squeezes. He doesn't understand why she's leaving with him, but he won't ask. They pass by the cokeheads and make their way out of the door.

# Lena

### Nairobi, Kenya, July 2002

'The roads were so clean. You wouldn't believe it. Never seen anything like it. Not in London, nor Portugal, nor anywhere else I've been. It was like no one dared to break the rules,' she said.

'I can understand that,' Kojo said. 'They don't want disorder of any kind. Not now. The Rwandans have been through so much, and it's very recent history. Not even ten years ago.'

'And the contrast with Congo, well...' She tried to describe it, but the words in her head disappointed her. So she took out her digital camera and showed him some photos she'd shot of Goma town. Also the roads in Bunia. She enjoyed recounting the jokes of Abbé Augustin and the stories about the water projects supporting the peacebuilding. She didn't tell him about the time she wrenched open the car door on the muddy hillside. The anxiety so deep she could have drowned in it. You can't describe that kind of frantic feeling, you just have to try to forget it. She never mentioned Abbé Augustin's story about his friend, even though she couldn't stop thinking about the car sliding off the cliff.

The roads in Nairobi were flowing with traffic moving at a satisfying pace, and there was a buzz around the businesses, the malls, the markets. Kojo didn't have time to take her around to show her these places, but a driver gave her a short tour on the way back to the accommodation she would share with Kojo and four other staff members.

She was surprised to see that the place was very modern, with an updated kitchen, a cook, and a swimming pool. She missed the simplicity of the villa in Angola, where she and Kojo had met and fallen in love. She couldn't explain why. It was a broken-down place without a running shower or a working toilet, but she had loved it. Things had been basic and she'd accepted it. It was simple, yet you had what was important.

But she'd adjust to being here. Ever since she was a child she had wanted to live with a pool. Or by the ocean, but a pool was a close second. No chance of that in London, but here, life was different. You were entitled to a bit of space, maybe, if you worked for it.

That night, she crept into Kojo's room. If he wasn't expecting it, he should have been. She had been away from him too long, needed his body next to hers. They made love slowly, silently.

Afterwards, she placed her hand inside his palm, swirling her finger around like she was telling his fortune. There was very little light, but she could feel the lines in his palms, also felt the hardened spots.

'You still have them, then?' she whispered. 'Your callouses, from plumbing the refugee camps?'

'It wasn't so long ago. Maybe five, six weeks since I was there last.'

'I wonder how long you'll hold onto them?'

'Who says they'll go?'

'I thought people went soft, if they gave up the hard labour.'

'They're a part of me. Have been for a long time. I don't think I'm going to soften up that much.'

'Hope not,' she said, although she didn't really know what she meant by that.

After a few minutes, she said, 'You know, Kigali? In 1994?'

'You want to talk about genocide before going to sleep?'

'No, it's just… I don't know if I could work there. Knowing all that happened. And learning some history, about how the UN and others failed to stop it.'

He exhaled. 'It's complicated.'

'I know, and how can we understand it? We weren't there.'

'Even the people who were there didn't understand it. Some of the world's greatest aid workers, journalists, photographers were there and tried to document it, tried to intervene. Later quite a few of them had breakdowns… It was such a traumatic time.'

'Does CWW do a lot of work there?'

'Don't worry, I'll send you to other assignments, at least starting off.'

'You're giving me an assignment at this time of night?'

'Let's talk tomorrow…'

'Love you.'

'Love you too.'

# Nine

**Bene**

It's a relief to be back outside. Fatima doesn't drop his hand as they walk across the square. He wants to look up and wave to Gabriel and his phony friends, but that would be showing off. Still, he hopes they are watching.

The singer in the square is taking a moment between songs to adjust his microphone. Fatima wants to stop to see what might come next. But the piano player starts a conversation with a beautiful woman, and doesn't seem in any hurry to finish. The singer keeps fiddling, then stops to flip through music on a wobbly wire stand.

Without words, they agree to move on. She takes him back to the metro stop, but then they walk further. There is suddenly a large boulevard with an amazing view of the Eiffel Tower.

'Don't you want to climb it?' she asks.

'I was there today,' he says. He drops her hand to slip off his backpack and take his notebook out to show some drawings from the afternoon.

'The pillar. I like it.' She says it like she really does.

'It's nothing, just a sketch.'

'You'll be a great architect, you know that, right?'

He shakes his head. He hasn't proved anything, not yet.

She flashes a smile at him. 'Come, I want you to meet my sister.'

He doesn't feel like going back into another party with people he doesn't know, but she says her sister will change his mind. She seems really keen that they meet. They are somewhere in north Paris – they take the metro to Clichy. Where the hell is Clichy? He can't let himself get too lost, has to make his way back by midnight.

'It won't take long,' she says. They've gone off the edges of the central-Paris map in his head, and she pulls him through streets that feel very different. They are no longer so straight, so manicured. And they haven't seen a musician in ages. He wishes they were back in the centre of town where he can be sure of making his way back to the hostel if everything ends badly.

There is some great graffiti. He stops to take out his camera, but she hisses back to him, 'Not here!'

He apologises.

She stops in the middle of a block. There is music coming from behind a garage door. She types in the code numbers and then slides the door up and over her head. Inside the garage space are six or seven scooters, parked haphazardly. 'My brothers,' she says, gesturing to the bikes. 'And their friends.' He wonders how many kids there are in her family. There are so many things she hasn't told him yet.

They walk across a courtyard, and she knocks on a patio door on the ground floor. Someone pulls back the curtains and looks out, a face in shadow with long dark curls like Fatima and an orange glow from a cigarette.

'They can be a bit crazy, you know...' Fatima says, reaching for his hand. 'But they're lovely people, you'll see.'

The woman opening the door holds her cigarette away from them and blows out smoke to the side. 'So, you're the new friend? *Ça va?*' She kisses him on the cheek three times, not giving him a chance to reply. 'I'm Aisha.'

'And you are... Fatima's twin sister?' He tries to get a smile.

'That's very sweet. But not to her. I have had so many wrinkles already she wouldn't want to match my face for my worries. I'm six years older. We have a brother in between. And a younger one too. You'd like them...' She looks over her shoulder.

Fatima whispers something in Aisha's ear then leads Bene into a kitchen. It's a narrow room, every surface covered with plastic cups, wine bottles, crisp packets, and containers of hummus and other foods. The smell is of sesame and cigarette smoke. He realises he hasn't eaten since he left the hostel hours ago.

There is drumming and singing coming from the next room. 'They always do this,' Fatima says, as she opens the door. In a circle there are something like fifteen people, with more on the fringes, sitting on couches or beanbags or just the floor. Some have instruments like hand drums and cymbals. Others have overturned pots or saucepans. They use metal utensils, cooking spoons or hands to hit every available possible surface. The clicks and clattering of metal, wood and plastic, of people's rings, of jangling bracelets, make a steady rhythm with all sorts of interesting harmonies and clashes. Most of the people have their eyes shut, although a few look up and nod when Fatima brings him into the room. Some chant in a language he doesn't understand, others hum or just make notes with their voices, not saying any particular words but blending sounds together.

'Here.' Fatima gives him a small pot and a wooden spoon. The underside of the pot is dented already, from earlier drum circles like this, he imagines. It is still warm from someone else's hands.

He crosses his legs and sits with her, just outside the circle. Starting to play, he finds a steady beat in the middle of it all, holding it together –

the pulse. Everyone is essentially dancing their rhythm around that central one. They add extra flourishes, a rat-a-tat here or extra pizazz there. An improvised off-beat there, and then they come back to that essential rhythm, pulsing through. It never ends, just morphs into something else, agreed without words with the whole crowd.

Time passes, and Bene's legs start to tingle from sitting cross-legged for so long, but he doesn't want to stop. He feels a joy he hasn't felt in a long time. Like music is coming out of him, going somewhere significant. Contributing to something bigger and more powerful than himself, he feels found.


'You've never been to Nairobi before?'

He wishes he hadn't said anything. A sophisticated woman like her, she would see through his travel plans for what they were: blindly flying in the dark. Obviously risking a huge disaster when he gets there, not thinking about that bit.

'But your father, he's not taken you to Ghana or anywhere?'

'Never met him. I don't even think he knows I exist.'

She blows out her cheeks as if she lacks the words to comment. She probably can't imagine life without a ring of family around her. The rhythm from the drum circle continues in the living room, but they came outside when she gestured she needed a break. The fresh air makes him miss the ocean for a moment, doesn't know why.

'But you're heading out there?'

'Mum was supposed to come too, but then her friend in London got sick. She's coming later, but there's another lady who's going to pick me up. I dunno...' It is starting to sound really stupid.

'She didn't say anything to him?'

'How would I know? Anyway, a guy's got to meet his father, doesn't he?'

'I'm sure if you're worried about it, you could talk it through.' She holds out her mobile to him. 'Do you want to call your mum?'

He pushes the phone back down into her lap, leaves his hand on top of hers. 'Naw, I think she's busy.'

She lets him keep his hand there, hers warm and still.

'No stars,' he says, looking up above the buildings.

'Course not. Light pollution, *non*?'

'Shame. If you came to Funchal you'd see such beautiful stars over the ocean.'

'Wish I was there now.'

'With me, I hope.'

'With you.' She turns in to kiss him. For a perfect moment that is all he is: feeling her soft lips and her textured tongue sending tingles and signals shooting through his mind and body like fireworks. It's the best feeling of his life.

.

# Part II

# Ten

## Lena

### London, 22 June 2022

She wonders if Lucian knows she is there. He breathes calmly with the help of the machine, and she hopes the tube isn't too uncomfortable. The heart monitor continues its faithful beeping. There's something reassuring in that.

Why doesn't he wake up? The doctors said he should be awake by now. The surgery was yesterday; they removed some of the tissues in his throat but not his larynx. Chemo and radiation will follow, if he can handle it. Why didn't he seek treatment earlier? Probably just thought it was a cough from the pollution. Lucian always seemed invincible, somehow, in that streetwise way of his. But he didn't have a wife to remind him to get himself checked out.

He is her oldest friend, the only one from home who has followed her trajectory from London to Africa and then back to Madeira to nest. Like a bird, he used to tell her, in the short emails and chats they'd have. He couldn't understand why she never moved back to where she grew up, with him.

He always had such a continuous, sarcastic edge about him. As if nothing could bother him. Nothing would move him without his grudging consent. Still lives in the same flat in Stockwell, for God's sake.

There's a flutter around his eyelashes. A positive sign. She squeezes his hand, hoping he can sense her there.

He doesn't look like himself. He is wearing the hospital gown, and his hair, thinning into blond-grey wisps, falls back from his forehead. Someone ought to give him a shampoo. His face sinks into the pillow. He was always skinny – that was just his body shape. Now gravity is conspiring to make him seem even thinner, and it scares her.

How long has it been? Some months since they had a video call over WhatsApp, and Lucian was amazed at the size of Bene. Already a teenager, nearly a man. She doesn't know why she has never brought him to London to meet Lucian in person. It never seemed to be the right time. There's so much to show Bene, but it's really hard to find a way to explain it all to him. How do you talk about the divide between your life before you became a mother, and everything you've been through since?

Bene. Even as she worries at her friend's bedside, her thoughts go to mothering. It's such a strange feeling. You can give birth to someone. Raise him as best you can. Watch him grow these long legs and big ideas, become argumentative and creative and kind and impatient, all in a blur of days and years. It passes so fast you don't have time to notice or document it properly. And then he is grown. Taking his own photos, making his own moves.

But you are so used to being with him, you still talk to him, in your head, all the time. You make an observation and try to say something to him. You turn around and he's nowhere near. You are torn between trying to remember it for later, and chiding yourself that the little details don't need to be shared anymore.

And you remember that you gave him a plane ticket.

And then you let him go.

# Kojo

**Nairobi, 22 June 2022**

He likes the view of the courtyard before dawn, once he unlocks the window bars. Even though he's been there for decades, he'll never get used to the number of locks he needs to do up each evening and morning. He has to unlock their bedroom. Then the gate at the staircase. Then downstairs, the kitchen door from the hallway. And then the kitchen windows, and the back door. He feels like a caged animal. Amazing how the level of crime has come to this.

But he knows he is a privileged man. Not yet sixty years old and very healthy. Uses the gym four mornings a week, comes back home for breakfast with Paradisa and Omondi before work.

The way he sees it, maybe God decided against giving him children of his own. He works long hours, and has never settled down with a wife. But God decided to put children into his life.

Kojo directs large-scale humanitarian projects that impact on hundreds of thousands of families across Africa. Over the years, he has helped reach millions of children. But also, Omondi is special. He is so smart. Eight years old and asking questions about astronauts and the universe. He memorised the flags of every country in the world. He reads with a torch after lights-out, like any inquisitive child would do.

He remembers Omondi when the two of them first moved in. He was small like a frightened baby steenbok, with eyes that seemed to be much bigger than they were supposed to be. Impossibly skinny legs, bruised shins and shoes without laces. Kojo took care of that. He went out and bought the boy a new pair of school shoes right away. Bought the whole uniform. It wasn't much. And he started paying the school fees. Somebody had to look after the boy.

Paradisa cleaned for Kojo for months before she shared with him the story of Omondi's father rejecting them, convinced that Omondi was another man's child. Kojo, whose large compound is provided by his position at CWW, listened sympathetically, and said she could take the flat on the ground floor.

Paradisa still calls him Mr Appiah, and he's stopped trying to get her to use his first name. When she knocked on his bedroom door that night, he was only half-surprised. She wanted to lie with him. He made it clear to her that she didn't have to. But she took to this habit of coming into his bed. With her long white nightgown, and her hair wrapped in the traditional scarf from up north. She lies in his bed and says nothing. Then when he switches the light out, she turns over and wraps her arms around him in a tight hold until her breathing slows.

He doesn't mind. He found it amusing at first, endearing. Now he's quite used to it. When it happens, he closes his eyes and pretends to sleep too. Her hold relaxes, then he can open his eyes and look at her. Her mouth slightly open, her breath moist and smelling of toothpaste. She has a worried look on her face, even when she sleeps. He has no idea what she is thinking. Often she shouts out in her sleep. But it is in a local language from her village up north, and he is not meant to understand. She uses him as a physical presence against some demons in her unconscious. To his surprise, he is fine with being used in such a way. It's better than being alone.

The mobile phone is ringing. He takes it from the kitchen charger and is puzzled; he knows this is not his day for being on call. He looks at the clock, and it says 5:30 am. It's his oldest friend, Jeanette. They worked together in Angola fifteen years ago and followed each other's promotions and changes with an understanding of colleagues more devoted to work than anything else.

'Kojo, wake up,' she says.

'What's wrong? Are you okay?'

'I'm fine, but there's something I need to tell you.'

'Now?'

'It's about my visitor, the one I told you about. The boy I wanted you to meet.'

'Jeanette, why are you calling me now?' He looks through the kitchen door at the stairs, hoping his voice doesn't wake Omondi.

'Kojo, he didn't get off the plane. They said he didn't board it in Paris.'

'Call him. You have a mobile number?'

'Not answering. His mum's neither.'

'What do you want me to do about it?'

'Help me, I need to track him. He's my responsibility you see...'

He doesn't understand why she is so upset. 'Wait a minute, Jeanette. Let me make some coffee. I'll ring you right back, and we'll figure out what to do.'

Jeanette, like him, was unmarried; what family she has is back in Ireland, and there isn't anyone else to rely on. He knows they serve that role for each other. Humanitarians tend to gravitate within the orbit of each other, but many never quite commit.

He's grateful for what he has – a solid reputation, good friends, a steady job and a pension secured. For what he doesn't have, he's not someone who focuses too much on what didn't happen. It isn't a wise man who tries to walk ahead in life looking backwards.

# Eleven

**Lena**

**London, 22 June 2022**

She turns and nearly falls out of the cot onto the hospital floor. Damn, these things are narrow. They're not intended for long-term comfort. Just a short reprieve for worrying relatives at the bedside of someone they care about.

It's not even 7 am. If Lucian were healthy, and in his flat at home, there's no way he'd be awake at this time. She can risk going to get a coffee from the vending machine.

She sees herself in the mirror. She looks old. The greenish lighting doesn't help. The woman scowling back has dry, wrinkled skin and looks permanently worried. How did it come to this?

Bene – she remembers his flight plans. He should be landing soon. She looks at her mobile and remembers that the nurses asked her to switch it off during the night. Never mind. It's on now and he'll text when he's ready. She can't remember if the time difference is two or three hours at this time of year.

She finds the vending machine and sits down with a paper cup of awful but just-this-side-of-tolerable coffee. When was the last time she was in a hospital? Bene has been such a healthy kid, it hasn't been too often, thank God.

Aunt Magda's scare last year, that was alarming. A woman like her, she's such a physically active person you can't imagine her stopping work. Magda's been repairing sails for longer than Lena has been alive. Her broad arms sweep the ungainly things through the industrial-sized sewing machines in the boatshed at the back. What would they do without Magda? Thankfully it wasn't a stroke. Not yet. That's what the doctor said to them. It was a joke he and Magda liked, and they kept chuckling about it. *Not yet.*

The other times in hospital – Bene's birth, so long ago. Before that, it was here, actually. This same hospital in South London twenty years ago. The roles were reversed, though. She was in the hospital bed, Lucian holding vigil and drinking the disgusting coffee. Her malaria was in retreat, all the indicators looked good. But then bleeding started. She hadn't even known she was pregnant but there was so much blood. Lucian said little, but stayed with her the whole time, looking scared and overwhelmed at the forces beyond his control. He left the room every twenty minutes to smoke another cigarette and then came back by her side. For once she didn't say anything about the ever-present smell of smoke.

Usually she waved him away when he got too close. But that time, she needed him near. She had no one else.

# Kojo

### Nairobi, 22 June 2022

Jeanette looks shaken. Her two plaits, normally down to her shoulders, are twisted left and right like pipe cleaners. Her makeup is smudged as if she has only snatched a bit of sleep, face-down, on some borrowed surface.

'We'll find him, don't worry.' Kojo gives her a hug as she gets into his car. 'Let's take you back to the airport and find this boy.'

She starts crying. She tries to keep it quiet but that leads to the opposite effect of her gasping for air and gulping the tears down. It would have been comical, except she is his closest friend. But he doesn't understand the anguish.

His attention stays on the traffic. It is moving, for once, and he needs to stay alert. You never know with Nairobi, whether it will be gridlocked or fluid. It is made up of constantly moving pieces, like a puzzle or video game, with different-sized shapes trying to jam into spaces not big enough for all of them.

He listens as her breathing slows back down, seeing in his peripheral vision that she stares straight ahead.

'Jeanette, he's a teenager, right? He was probably partying and missed a plane. Or got locked out of the hostel after losing his passport. Or got bumped onto another flight. You know Air Portugal is rubbish at last-minute changes.'

'I know, I know... but you don't understand... If something happened to him...'

'Who is this kid? I didn't know you had a nephew or someone who could make you so worried.'

'Kind of a nephew, it was going to be a surprise, you see...'

'What do you mean?'

She hesitates, which is so unlike her that his concentration slips from the driving. Usually she jumps right in and fills the air with whatever story was entertaining her recently, or long ago. To Jeanette, friendship means sharing whatever is on your mind, in whatever fashion the words tumble out. But this seems to be different.

'Kojo,' she says, 'it's your son.'

He hears the words but does not understand. He has to keep looking forward. It is a tricky roundabout with beggars, hawkers, cars and matatus all trying to merge and gain on each other.

They clear the roundabout with only a few horns hooting, and he comes back to what she just said. She must have misspoken. Maybe she wants a son, but never mentioned it before now? She's clearly upset.

'I don't have a son,' he says slowly. 'Do you mean to tell me you are thinking of adopting a child? Is that what this is about?' He can feel her eyes on him. Heat rises up his neck to his ears and his temples.

'No, he's not mine,' she says.

She must be confused. Maybe the stress of work has caught up with her. He makes a mental note to look again at her workload and suggest some R&R again before too long. 'Jeanette, what are you saying?'

'She told me a month ago. I had no idea before then. She swore me to secrecy.'

'She, who?' he asks, but he knows the answer. He doesn't want to think back to the past. But Jeanette's forcing the issue. He starts to feel angry, wants to get out of the car before he says something he'll regret. He doesn't like this old feeling of fury crawling up the back of his throat. It's not the kind of man he is. He is a calm man. The leader of CWW for all of Africa. He has achieved so much, on his own. He can't afford for it all to fall apart.

# Twelve

## Lena

### Khartoum, Sudan, July 2003

She still loved it. Flying over and into a new country. Cramming through her last-minute notes before touching down.

She was an outsider, and wanted to learn everything. She drenched herself in new information and absorbed it all. She had never been to Sudan before, in her year of roaming East Africa and the Horn of Africa working for CWW's regional office. She was flying into a new situation to the west of the country, a fact-finding mission of sorts.

CWW had been worried about the reports of large-scale displacement happening in Darfur, on the border with Chad. No reporters were allowed in. Word-of-mouth talked about men on horseback, called the *Janjaweed*, attacking people and forcing whole villages to flee. They sounded like menacing characters from a poem by Lewis Carroll, but apparently they were very real indeed. The Khartoum government, hardened by years of civil war in the south, was already deploying scorched-earth tactics in this new conflict. Satellite imagery showed that they were using these fighters as mercenaries while bombing villages from above.

It was a growing humanitarian crisis. Was CWW needed in this context? That was her job to assess. Was she qualified to do so? No one seemed to ask that question, nor focus too much on her security training or emergency procedures. Kojo taught her a few things about self-defence and identifying a proof-of-life safe word. But, of course, they prayed she would never have to use it.

She was happy being the scout. She was used to the weight of her cameras, wearing the vest with pockets for her notebook, film canisters and extra batteries. She always had more than one pen, in case one ran out of ink. She wrote notes in shorthand, which, along with her terrible handwriting, was a safe kind of code. Emergency chocolate bars and nuts for energy were also squirrelled away in that vest for when a quick energy shot was needed.

She felt strong and useful for all the time that she'd been part of the CWW team. She couldn't imagine being anywhere else. She had caught it – the passion for humanitarian work that gripped people and didn't let go.


The city of Khartoum was dusty and quiet. It was Ramadan so whatever restaurants there might have been were shuttered and closed. She was booked in at an inexpensive hotel frequented by UN personnel and NGOs. It had an alcohol-free bar draped with fake gold and moth-eaten rugs on the chairs and lining the floor. There were just take-away chicken drumsticks and out-of-date jars of tropical juice on offer. She'd chance it, she was that hungry.

The hotel was an old office block, converted without too much finery into rooms for a night. In the corridor the air conditioning units stuck out like mushrooms, heating the walkway with its walls and floors of unfinished concrete. Never mind, she was only spending a night or two there before flying to Darfur for a week. Just needed to sort out her internal visa. The government offices, normally closed, were open for a couple of hours for UN and expat staff only. She needed to be sure to be there.

# Kojo

### Nairobi, June 2003

Lena had been tracing a circle around a mole on his forearm while they planned the trip. They explored plans and bodies together, getting excited at both, dreaming of both, looking forward to the travel as well as the intimacy upon returning home. Kojo knew it was unorthodox – he was her manager, the planning should have been happening at a desk, not in bed. But that wasn't their way.

'I don't know any Arabic,' she said.

'Nor me. If you find that there's a job to do there, maybe we'll have to learn.'

'I'm not that hot at languages, I'm afraid.'

'Next you're going to tell me you're too old.' He glanced at where her hands were tracing and saw his veins under the surface. He stopped her movements and looked at her hands. She was fifteen years younger than him, and you could tell, from the hands. She still had some fullness there, protecting the ligaments and bone. For God's sake. What was such a young woman with all this potential doing with him?

It was the job, really. The situation. The passion that comes from having a shared focus. He'd seen it before: with colleagues who'd had that spark, but then it fizzled out when one of them got an office job, or the other wanted to move back closer to family. Family complicated things. They got older and had weddings or christenings and tried to pull you back towards them. But unless you had children yourself, you could just ignore the call of the mundane and have your adventures. Life felt ripe and full and exciting. You felt as if you were on the edge of history, as it was being made, in real time.

People were writing articles about the wars CWW was working in. Newspapers were running Lena's photos because they were too scared to send their own reporters. People would write books about it, but not yet. In the humanitarian phase, it was all so alive. Untranslated. Unmitigated. Raw. And there was so much to do.

In the bedroom, they unfurled the maps and tried to make sense of the terrain, the borders, the movements of people. They made lists in the air, recited them back to each other so they didn't forget. They talked about the destinations – Nyala first, then Al Fashir, possibly Geneina after – and agreed the criteria for making future choices. He made her memorise the phone numbers of the security emergency satellite phone as well as the SOS Air Ambulance.

They were the same, really. Born so far apart on different continents, they were both destined to be this: outsiders, observing, attempting to help in a fascinating sea of humanity's ups and terrible downs.

He loved the job. He loved Lena. He told her, as often as he could. Those were the two things he was clear about. Everything else fell to the side and mattered not at all.

# Thirteen

## Lena

### Nyala, Darfur (Western Sudan), August 2003

It was an ochre-coloured landscape. The vehicle shuddered with every crack in the road, weaving around potholes and gullies. The car wasn't a Land Rover, not even a 4x4. It was an old Toyota with no air conditioning or seatbelts. CWW had no staff here, and no partners. So Lena had no friends, no allies, no base; not yet.

Through a colleague in Nairobi she had contacted a small medical NGO who arranged a driver to meet her at the local airstrip. As they drove, windows down in the heat, Lena was coated with layers of sand and dust. She wore a light white shirt with long sleeves that fluttered in the wind. Even through her khakis, her legs stuck to the plastic seats. She didn't dare drink much water, in case there was a limited supply ahead. Despite sunglasses, she squinted with the overwhelming brightness of sun on thirsty and cracked land. It felt wide open and exposed, this corner of Sudan.

And it was hot, over 40 degrees. On the edge of the Sahel, the desert was never far away and could easily extend its grip further. Despite the temperature outside, the driver kept the heating blowing in the car. There hadn't been time to arrange an Arabic interpreter, but Lena soon worked out what was going on through gesture and the few words she and the driver shared: they needed to keep air flowing over the ancient engine, which rattled and jumped unpredictably. It was clear that no one would want to have the car break down in this heat.

When they came into built-up areas, he gently put his hand over the opening of her camera bag. 'No here,' he said. 'No good, no photo.'

She nodded and tried to understand what was unspoken. In the towns, people turned to see the car drive by. If they recognised the vehicle or the driver, they showed no sign. Donkeys moved to the side to let them past; women pulled cloths over their faces, disguising their expressions. Did they want to hide, or were they just shielding themselves against the sand and the dust? It was hard to interpret, in a place where she was so ignorant of both the language and the history.

It was a new and different feeling, being in the field ahead of the team. Everything needed to be negotiated and navigated very carefully. What steps she took or offences she accidentally made would ultimately reflect on CWW's ability to set up and work here.

She met with members of the medical NGO and arranged for a translator the next day. She stayed with the team at their compound, a broken-down former family home on the edge of Nyala. The building had hard edges of concrete blocks, unprotected against the encroaching desert. No one had painted it or cared for the premises in a long time. It had a rooftop for relaxing on after sunset, but perhaps since alcohol wasn't allowed, there wasn't the easy social atmosphere she was used to. The colleagues running the medical programme – a French logistician, a Kenyan doctor and two German nurses – seemed guarded, and they each ate dinner alone in their rooms.

In the morning, lingering over coffee, she managed to get one of the nurses to speak to her in some detail. Petra was a large white woman, with short hair that she might have cut herself in front of an imperfect mirror. She shifted in her seat as she spoke, and her skin was dark red along her collar where sunburn touched. Her lips were peeling from the dryness, and she kept biting them. She spun her spoon in her coffee cup with a vigour that threatened to chip the mug.

'I've worked in Indonesia, Ethiopia, Eritrea, Uganda... lots of tough places,' Petra said. 'I can take the restrictions, the curfews, the double-speak when the government says one thing, but then armed men do the opposite. I'm not a wimp. But it's so bad here, I don't know how long I can take it.'

Lena sat back and listened to the grievances that occupied Petra's mind. No water for showers, just sponge baths. No running toilet. No freedom to walk alone as a woman. Restrictions on where and when she could see patients. Soldiers knocking on the door at odd hours of night, threatening but then backing down. Patients arrested while standing in line to see the nurse. Flights of relief goods circling then failing to land. Airdrops of vital medical equipment dropped in the wrong location and smashed; relief supplies tampered with so they were useless when they finally reached IDP camps.

Underneath the stories, it seemed like an ongoing pattern of disruption and intimidation. The reasons behind the fighting and government crackdown in Darfur were known, but everything else seemed to be masked by layers of deception. She knew about a new rebel group rising up and attacking an army barracks last month. This was a humiliating defeat for the government in Khartoum. Not risking any more casualties, they counter-attacked from the air, bombing villages accused of harbouring the rebels. Then they also contracted the Janjaweed.

Lena wanted to know more about this mysterious army of men on horseback. Did they really exist?

Petra was adamant. 'I have seen them with my own eyes. We got a message from the army not to go to Geneina the last week of April. I felt imprisoned in the compound so I went to the rooftop in the early morning, before the sun was too hot. I could see in the distance these lines of men on horseback. They looked like a medieval army, advancing confidently with nothing to stop them. They kicked up so much dust you couldn't see the ground. They had scarves wrapped around their faces because they ride through the desert, and they never take them off. So, there's no identification, no retribution for their crimes.'

Petra paused to drink more coffee, still with the spoon inside, which came dangerously close to her eye. 'They are scary as hell. Rumour has it that they are mercenaries brought in from Chad. They don't speak the local language, and show no mercy. There's no reason to; they have no ties to the communities. It's not their mothers or sisters they are trampling with the hooves of those beasts...' She stared into the bottom of her mug.

Lena left a silence, to see if she wanted to say more.

'The people think they are ghosts,' Petra added. She cocked her head to the side to see if Lena would mock her. 'Phantoms or something. I think they are, or close to it. Angels of death, that's who they serve.'

Lena wondered if the woman had lost her perspective. No rational person would believe in ghosts.

Petra read her thoughts. 'You think I'm crazy, but you spend a few months here and then see what kind of mental state you are in.' She stood up abruptly, taking her coffee cup to the sink. 'We're all just one pace ahead of the shadows here. If you're not careful, they'll catch up with you, in the end.'

Over the course of the week, as Lena met with the other members of the team, the humanitarian picture started to emerge. Towns thought to be disloyal to the government were being attacked and razed. Camps for displaced people were assigned and villagers being pushed to go to them; yet it wasn't clear if there was any water, food or other services waiting for people in these camps. Perhaps they were being sent there to starve.

It took weeks and an inordinate amount of pressure on the authorities for humanitarian workers to register for long-term visas, which could be denied or withdrawn at any time. Petra and the others desperately wanted other agencies to come out too, to provide more services and to bear witness to what was happening. They felt raw and exposed, being the only international faces in what had turned into an active conflict far away from television cameras and the rule of law.

CWW could have a role to play in installing water and sanitation in these camps. But they wouldn't be able to work alone. Agencies needed permits to bring in food and nutrition supplements, and proper medical equipment. The terrain might call for deep-drilling equipment, and Lena knew from other assignments that this could be very costly. Even if they could free up the equipment from other missions, they could lose a lot of time trying to import it into Sudan. What other solutions had she spoken to the logistics team about? She racked her brain – she needed to speak to Kojo. Water bladders? Filled up from the wells in town and then trucked out to the camps? Could they hire lorries out here? Or maybe something more basic, like donkeys, could do the trick. Some kind of water-caravan? She liked the idea.

But what were these IDP camps? Were they holding people, protecting them from military operations, as the army said? Or was it something more sinister? She couldn't afford to be naïve here. If she was going to make recommendations for CWW to take risks, and invest time, people and money in coming into Darfur, she had to get the analysis right.

She still had the feeling that she was missing the real story. She was making this up as she went along, this job of photographer/communications expert. But in a place like this, she hadn't felt comfortable taking many photos. People seemed to be suspicious of the camera, as if they knew something Lena didn't about the uses and abuses of images. Her vague promise to bring in more help meant little, compared to their certainty.

# Kojo

### Nairobi, September 2003

He took the satellite call from Lena in Nyala. He heard how upset she was and let her talk, even though it cost four dollars a minute.

He knew he had taken a risk, sending her out to scout ahead. But he didn't have many staff members, and he trusted her powers of observation over anyone's, possibly even his own. He'd tried to teach her the basics of CWW operations and the principles of water and sanitation; they worked in the intersection between water and simple measures of public health. She learned everything, forgot little. He was constantly impressed and a bit envious of her ability to dive into these subjects that were very different from anything in her previous experience. She always had the unconscious confidence of someone in the flow of action.

She told him about the camps in Darfur: that despite the announcements from the government, they were not really established. There were nearly no NGOs, the UN was restricted to just the big cities, and the water and sanitation services were non-existent. The medical NGO was very concerned about the potential for disease to break out and spread with the movements of large numbers of people into these unprepared camps.

There were protection issues too: women had to walk long distances to fetch drinking water and firewood, leaving behind their children in flimsy shelters. The women were putting themselves at risk of rape or worse, but they had no choice. In their absence, the children could get recruited by the rebels, or killed or kidnapped by the Janjaweed.

'I think they're being rounded up, Kojo,' Lena said.

'Are you in a safe space, Lena?'

'Why, no one can tap a sat phone, can they?'

'You could be overheard.'

'I'm back at the compound; no one is around but the cook.'

'Make sure he doesn't listen in. Sudan is notorious for sub-context.'

'Kojo, you should have seen these women. Most of them were too scared to talk to me. They refused to have their photo taken, too scared to have any proof that they were speaking to me. Petrified. I've never seen anything like it.'

Now that he heard her voice, satisfied that she was alright, he wanted to get her off the expensive phone call. 'Well, it sounds as if you're doing the job we set out for you to do, Lena. The team will be pleased to have such detailed observations.'

'I'm not finished yet. The team I went with, you know, from MedRef? They're scared too. At the last camp, they wanted to stop my attempts at interviewing, and pulled all the staff into a meeting without me.

'I can understand where they're coming from,' she continued. 'It's a delicate balance here to be seen as impartial and neutral, and people are afraid I'll mess it up. But I have never seen people so on edge. Not in Angola, Congo, Kenya, Rwanda... and there's more. There was also this feeling of aggression rising up. Anger at something. The idea that the NGOs could abandon them? Or something else, I don't know.

'Some of the men in the camp started posturing and pushing near a group of women I was talking to. Then the men circled around all of us women, and started chanting something. Quietly, almost imperceptibly, but definitely there.

'The interpreters said a few quick words to finish the meeting off and then all the ex-pats jumped into the cars and fled. My driver nearly left without me. The car was already rolling when I jumped inside.'

'Did they explain what was happening?'

'Apparently they thought we could be government informants. But I don't think that was the whole story. There was real hatred in their eyes. It was like I didn't matter; my foreignness, my presence was just dangerous or alien.'

'Well, take some time, write things down, we can interpret it all later when you are safely back.'

'There's something going on, Kojo. Something in the way of a wider conflict that is turning low-level skirmishes into something...'

'... Something?'

'Something I can't even imagine.'

'It's not like you to be so dramatic.' It came out harsher than he meant. She paused. He could hear her breathing.

'We almost hit someone, Kojo.'

'In the car?'

'Yes, an aid organisation supposed to be saving lives, and the driver was so panicked by the crowd that he nearly hit someone. A child. It was difficult driving, I give him a lot of credit for that. But it's clear there is a heightened fear here, Kojo. The drivers, the displaced people, the doctors. Fear mixed with anger and a strong feeling that the worst is yet to come.'

'You sound stressed. Let's get you home. Finish this mission, and we'll talk it through together.'

'Sure, yeah.' Another pause. 'You're better in person, anyway. Hard to talk over the phone.'

'You know how expensive calls are. Let's free up the phone and say goodnight, shall we?'

'Love you.'

'Yes. Of course. Me too.'

# Fourteen

## Lena

**London, 22 June 2022**

'You're back with us,' Lena says. She doesn't let go of Lucian's hand.

He doesn't look at her yet. She can see his eyelashes move as he blinks and focuses. He had a bad reaction to the anaesthetic; probably feels a bit out of sorts at the moment. His breathing is raspy but steady.

Will he be able to speak? The doctors weren't sure. It may take some therapy, and some luck. After all the thousands upon thousands of cigarettes he's smoked, it would take a bloody miracle.

He moves his head gently from side to side, as if to see if it's still attached. Then he stretches his fingers, and she drops his hand. She doesn't want to press him. He knows she is there, that's the main thing. That's why she left everything else, even being with Bene on his first trip to Africa. Lucian is her oldest friend. Their childhood seems not so much a different chapter but a separate existence altogether. Grown-up Lena can't remember what it felt like to be young Lena, or adolescent Lena. Londoner Lena. It's as if she had started out with a twin once, but lost her somehow.

'Fucking hell,' Lucian grumbles, and then starts to cough.

Lena gets up and flags the nurses that he's awake. She's really happy to have him back, swearwords and all. She listens to the doctors as they recount to Lucian how the surgery went. The cancer was not as widespread as it could have been. How the lucky bugger has got away with more than twenty-five years of smoking is a mystery.

# Kojo

### Nairobi, 22 June 2022

The phone is off. How could her phone be off? It's galling that the first and only time he tries to ring her after all these years, she has the nerve to ignore it.

How the hell could she not tell him he had a son? His whole professional life, he's been cut off from family, never had anyone. His parents died without knowing, thinking he failed the family. His brother Kumi – more successful in business, marriage and life – was the only one they honoured. Kumi's children in Accra – they have all the family inheritance and goodwill. Kojo himself was always alone, on another side of the continent, unattached and growing old.

They were together almost two years. She never mentioned wanting to have kids, never talked about settling down. Making a child with him? No, never came up. They would have laughed about it. Too preposterous an idea. Raising a child? While jumping in and out of Land Rovers in war zones? While going to nightclubs in Nairobi and then racing to the airport early the next morning? While watching the sun rise over the highway and the early vendors trying to sell their fruit, weaving around the stopped traffic? Impossible. Never would have happened.

They had been so excited about travelling, serving CWW, setting up new camps or making sure the established ones were running smoothly. Handling the media enquiries, getting her photos in the British or French press, online and across the world. Getting the grants for the new aid projects, going to scale in places where people desperately needed the water and sanitation. They worked together to get the stories out about critical needs and humanitarian access in a dozen countries across Africa. Stories that no one would have heard of if it weren't for her work.

They were getting the word out, making sure there were no more forgotten emergencies. When the television cameras and politician's attentions were distracted elsewhere, they made sure their stories hit the news.

They were making history, in their own way. As a couple they defied convention. They didn't need a mortgage or any long-term plan. They often didn't see each other for long stretches of time. They usually didn't speak when either one was on mission. They saw each other between trips, over staff meetings, or just in the intimate hours. They lived on caffeine and endorphins. Loved every minute.

He'd loved it. Hadn't she?


But she left. Left Nairobi. Left the job, left him. In such a hurry and without much of an explanation. Tears, yes, but his questioning was met with silence. She'd forgotten the language they used together, when they were intimate and on their own. How they could laugh and talk and discuss political events or just hold each other and listen to each other's breathing.

They stopped making love. It all fell apart, somehow, spectacularly but without any one event or reason. She left all that behind, and never came back.

He let her go. Didn't try to hold her back. Why? He can't remember the rationale now. It was strong in his head at the time. He was certain that it wasn't his fault, not his responsibility that things broke down. She was the one who made the move. Didn't even serve out her notice period. He knew she was a bit stressed out, but everyone in humanitarian work had to learn how to manage their emotions. That was part of the job.

Maybe they were too different, he had thought. Maybe she was too young for him. He figured maybe the pressure got to her, or she wanted something else.

The organisation needed him. They deserved a stable leader. Personal relationships were a distraction he could live without. After repeating it to himself often enough, over the months and years after she cut off all contact, he started to believe it.

And anyway, the work was overwhelming. Darfur's conflict was heating up just then, and he had teams rotating in and out of western Sudan on a rapid routine. They had to observe visa restrictions and strict safety protocols after threats to humanitarian workers reached a peak. Congo was still quite volatile, and he had to manage the teams there, as well as developing new programmes in response to drought and failed harvests in the east the following year. That was before Kenya's political violence in 2011, the time when there were riots close to his door in Nairobi.

And it was before he hired Paradisa, and met little Omondi. Before he bought that first pair of school shoes, for a boy who has no blood ties to him whatsoever.

But now, so many years later, he is desperate to get hold of the woman who slipped away. How could she tell Jeanette, a mere friend, and fail to tell the father of her child?


As they wait at the airport for the next flight from Paris, Jeanette gives him a large envelope with photos of a boy at different ages. At first, there is a photo of a teenager. He is a light-skinned, mixed-race child with short twists. Lena lets him grow his hair? Kojo has to smile. He had wanted hair like that when he was growing up, but his father had forbidden it. Asante pride in appearances, that was the lecture. No twists allowed.

Kojo hasn't had the chance to lecture anybody. He looks at the face. A handsome boy, turning into a man. Doesn't look familiar though. Not an obvious match. Maybe there, around the eyes. Something about his brother Kumi in there – mischief at the corners. And the shape of the face. The boy looks more like Lena's family, the Portuguese genes coming through.

Other photos – a toddler, the same child, but much chubbier and the eyes are outsized on the younger face. Another, a holiday snap, the boy must be only about eight years old and beams at the camera, holding a child-sized surfboard. The sea behind him is turquoise and calm. Is that the kind of life she's given him? Doesn't look too bad a place to grow up.

Then he is knocked back by a photo of a baby, maybe three months old, being held in Lena's arms. She looks exactly as he remembers her: young, flawless, natural. Her skin is paler and is framed by a fringe of black hair. Her face is the perfect oval with strong cheekbones that used to become more prominent when she was arguing a point.

But he has never seen her like this – maternal, caretaking. Holding a small precious person, a stranger to him. The child's eyes are wide and brown, but the skin is pale and he is bundled up in winter European clothes. He looks nothing like how an African boy would look.

She doesn't seem as if she's made for it, for being a mother. He remembers her at total ease in the field. Wearing two cameras strapped in an X across her body, she was ready for anything. In case of battery failure or a computer disaster, she had backup in the pockets of that photojournalist vest. She could fit a notepad in there besides, and wrote in a shorthand that only she could decipher. Her highest priority was ensuring she got the photos, and covered the material fairly and compassionately.

Seeing her like that in a photograph, it's like one of Omondi's books of safari animals. Mix and match. Where you can switch one animal's face with another animal's body or feet. A zebra's head with a lion's body, that sort of thing. Kojo bought it for the child soon after he moved in, thought it would make him laugh. But serious child that Omondi is, he just gave Kojo a curious look as he flipped all the possible combinations. Seemed to think there was something to figure out, about switching and matching these animal features.

What happened to Lena? Why did she say nothing?

He turns over the baby photo. It's dated December 2004.

# Fifteen

**Lena**

**London, 22 June 2022**

'Do you think I could get out of here for a fag?'

'You bastard. How can you say that after what we've been through? Taking your own sweet time coming out of the anaesthetic...' Lena stops when she sees the smirk on Lucian's face. He just wanted to know if she would launch into a motherly lecture.

'I was taking the mick, Lena. No desire ever to touch my lips to the filthy things again. They've given me a patch, see.' He gestured to his upper arm. His voice was gravelly and unfamiliar. But the rhythm and meaning of his speech were pure Lucian. She is grateful to have him back and teasing her. He always knew how to wind her up.

'You just see to getting better.' She swats him on the leg and he flinches. Maybe she underestimated her strength.

'I have a few voicemails... just a sec.' She steps out of the room into the corridor.

*Next of kin.* She hasn't heard that phrase in so long, more than twenty years. She never imagined it in relation to her son. That's wrong. They've got it wrong. There must be some mistake. The message from the airline doesn't say anything else, just informing her that he missed the flight from Paris.

Before she calls the number of the airline, she rings Bene's mobile. It goes straight to voicemail. Is it off? Why would it be turned off? Unless the battery went dead. Did he lose his phone? Or is he on a plane now? But the airline would know that, surely.

She paces the hallway for a second time in twenty-four hours, leaving a message for Bene telling him to ring her right away and explain why he missed his flight. Then she hangs up, annoyed with herself for the shrill tone in her voice, now permanently recorded to greet her son in a foreign country.

She just needs to know he's okay. She rings back, calmer this time. It goes again to voicemail. Maybe he's on the phone, trying to reach her? She leaves a second message, one with a softer and more understanding voice. She just wants to know he's alright; they'll get him on the next flight to Nairobi, no problem. Just ring.

She looks again at her phone, willing him to call. There are a number of missed calls. She goes through the list and sees that Jeanette tried to ring – shit, she's waiting in Nairobi with no information. And there's another Kenyan mobile she doesn't recognise.

She swallows hard.

This isn't how she wanted Kojo to find out. This isn't the conversation she wanted to have with him. She wanted to be there, with Bene, and the boy would smooth it over, as he always does.

That child has a natural grace and humour about him, always has had it. She knows that as his mother she was biased, but even when he was a schoolboy she'd seen how he could put people at ease, although he seemed completely unaware of the effect he had on them. He would read a situation as he entered it; in the first moment, he breathed in people's perfume of hopes and desires and somehow managed to say just the right thing. He would pluck the topic out of the air, the question to get people – young and old – talking, laughing, and relaxed in his presence.

It was a talent Bene had. She couldn't put her finger on what it was, or how he'd learned it. When he was younger, and confided in her in his trusting way, she tried to get him to name it. What was this, the ability to comfort people, even if they didn't know they needed comforting? He couldn't explain it, though. He grew shy when it was pointed out. Thought it was just a natural way of interacting. Or maybe he was embarrassed that she had to ask.

Where did it come from? Not from her. She wasn't graceful like that. Even at the best of times her few friends would say she was awkward and found it hard to predict people's reactions. She was blunt, that's what it was. Nothing to be ashamed of, but nothing to be proud of, either. Didn't make friends very easily, especially when she was unsure of herself. Maybe Bene is the way he is to make up for her faults. He compensates for her, and she is thankful for that.

He has graces and gifts that she herself didn't give him. Either he's absorbed them from the Madeira island air, or they came from his Ghanaian line.

She doesn't know what to say to Kojo. She should have thought this through. She was depending on Jeanette and Bene. She didn't predict that the plan would go awry. For goodness' sake, this wasn't how she wanted their first conversation to be like. The first in eighteen years.

She pretends to herself that she hasn't kept track of the time. She'd found it much harder in the beginning, when she was alone and heading to Madeira without a plan. Unforgivable, what she'd done. She still doesn't know why she did it. And why she found it impossible to change her mind once she had decided her course.

It was another life, the one they lived together. Kenya, Darfur, Congo, the missions and the plane flights and the night life and the late nights. The friendships with colleagues, and the intimacy that was theirs alone.

She had regrets, of course she did. She used to ring his land line when she knew he was out, just to hear his voice on the machine. She hung up every time before leaving a message. All the same, it amazed her how long he kept that message unchanged. He left it that way for years.

She had to turn all those feelings off, once Bene arrived and the decisions were made. Each decision cascaded from the previous one, as the baby came into her life. She had to acquire a birth certificate, a passport, an education. She left the father's name blank every time.

Indefensible, she knew. But the shaking, the nightmares, the overpowering reactions to large noises and small risks only started to subside when she threw herself into this new role called motherhood. When she focused all her energy on another person, this small and precious cargo she was now responsible for. She was finally being constructive rather than documenting other people's pain and destruction. She didn't have to have all the answers for impossible questions about why the UN didn't act, why military operations targeted women and children. Why the people she interviewed were in mortal danger but she could walk away. She didn't have to justify the past or make excuses for anyone.

She just looked forward, day by day. She wasn't sure if she was any good at it. There was no one to help guide her except her late father's sister; Aunt Magda had been living alone in Funchal, until Lena's request came from abroad. But Lena had instinct, and she felt that she could do it, if she detached herself from everything that came before.

Now that Bene stands on his own feet and has turned into such a lovely young man, she can trust him, more than anyone else. More than herself. He has the best of her, without her past or any of her mistakes. He seems to have sidestepped all that and come up with a personality that is all his own: enthusiastic, artistic, and quietly determined.

Why doesn't he answer his phone?

She doesn't expect forgiveness for her actions. She doesn't expect friendship or kindness or anything else. She doesn't know Kojo now, and probably only knew a fraction of who he was then, when they were together.

She just feels that she owes this to Bene, to help him tie the strands of his identity together. To understand more about the elements that are at play inside himself, his character and his potential, in life going forward.

Oh, it's all so stupid now, in the cold light of day. She doesn't know how she could have messed it up so badly. She wishes she knew someone who had the sense to know how to fix it.

Before listening to any other messages, she rings Bene's mobile again. This time it rings just once and then a woman's voice says, '*Bonjour*? Hello? *Merde.*'

Lena looks at her phone, assessing that she has dialled correctly. 'Who is this? Where's Bene?'

'*Oui,* yes this is Bene's phone.' The woman sounded young, French, and upset. '*Ç'est qui*?' Some ruffling on the French side. 'Oh, *c'est* "Mum". Is this Bene's Mum? Oh, *mon Dieu,* thank God.'

Lena doesn't have to say anything, she knows something is wrong with her son and that this girl, on the end of the line, needs her to play the mother role. 'What's happened to Bene?' she asks.

The girl explains in fast, frantic English something about a fight and a hospital. 'It all happened so fast, *madame.* I tried to stop it, before it got out of control. My sister's husband, ex-husband, started arguing and throwing things. Bene tried to calm it down, but he got hurt – I'm so sorry, it was an accident...'

115

'How hurt? Is he okay? Can't I speak to him?'

'That's the problem, *madame*.' The girl is crying now, gasping at her words and becoming harder to understand. 'We called an ambulance, but he lost a lot of blood and he's not speaking.' More crying and she takes several breaths before she continues. 'How do you say it? He's not awake. He won't wake up.'

'He's unconscious? Are you there with him?'

'No, *madame*. He is in surgery. The glass bottle smashed when it hit his head. There was so much blood, we tried to stop the bleeding, but I don't know if we did it right.' She descends into muffled sniffs and sobs.

'Where are you? I'm coming, right away.'

# Kojo

### Nairobi, 22 June 2022

He has so many questions for Jeanette, but he can't figure out how to ask them. The next flight from Paris arrives but there is no sign of this young man named Bene.

*Benedito*. How could Lena use that name? He knows it means blessed one, but the name is borrowed from a child who died a long time ago, on her first visit to Angola. One whose death they watched happen, together. How could she use that name, and imprint it onto her own flesh and blood? That couldn't be lucky, no matter what it means in translation. Kojo is not a religious man, but he has been around death so much that he knows it wisps around you, and takes hold wherever it likes.

You need to protect your children from that. Protection is the first thing you owe a child you bring into this world. Protect them and provide for them.

Jeanette says the boy is his son. And has photos to show his growing up, but what kind of proof is that? He doesn't even look Ghanaian.

Kojo doesn't feel anything for this teenager. What he feels, he has to admit, is for his mother. The photo of Lena. It's a face he hasn't looked at in what, eighteen years? He's not a man who holds onto photographs. He never takes them himself, only has the ones that are given as gifts or mementoes.

When Lena was with him, in Angola and Nairobi, she was rarely in the pictures, although she did put him in some of them. But he was never the star of the show. She knew her job – to document these humanitarian crises away from the spotlight. They had no photos taken of them together, he's fairly sure.

But God, how he'd missed her. Those early months when it was difficult to breathe. The sorrow hit him in the middle of his chest and he was worried that his heart might stop. But he could tell no one how it hurt; not Jeanette, not the team. He had to keep going in the pattern that defined him. Work on. Without her.

In the years that followed, her memory became blurred. He couldn't remember the distinct shape of her face. Her facial expressions, he couldn't say that he knew them anymore. Her body, too, had soft edges in his mind, then faded into nothing. The memory is a weak organ. Why are we so bad at remembering the sense of touch? The sense of smell? It's all gone, after a time. And we're left feeling empty, with nothing to show for two years of being intensely in love.


Jeanette comes back from the ladies' room, her makeup and hair slightly better arranged. He smiles at her. She has a kind face, an older face now. She has the permanent sunburned look, in the way that white people get after twenty years of working in Africa. She has spent the time smoking and paying little attention to her own health, despite being a highly trained nurse. And no matter the state of her complexion, her hair is always dyed a bright, magenta-red. Even when they lived in the outpost in the Angolan highlands, she managed to make it that colour. A hue not found in nature, other than perhaps in some rare tropical bird. That was her signature, made her stand out from other women. Whether for a laugh or for a statement, he has never asked.

Jeanette sees his smile and looks relieved. 'So you're too not angry, then?' she asks. She sits down next to him on the hard plastic chairs. The tannoy announces more flight arrivals, from Amsterdam, Johannesburg, and Dubai. Nothing from Paris.

'Angry, at the boy? For missing the plane and making you worry? Well...' He plays with his chin as if he had a beard. 'No, he's just a boy.'

'With me. For not telling you.'

'Yes, I considered that.' He pauses again. Where does anger come from, and where does it go? When you're a young man, you feel like you will burst if a decision goes the wrong way. He'd lost that, somewhere. That bolt-ahead-and-strike energy. He puts his head in his hands and runs his fingers over his smooth scalp. 'I don't know how you held it in, to be honest. Usually I can't stop you talking.'

She hits him lightly on the shoulder, and leaves her hand there.

'No, you had your reasons,' he continues.

'She only told me a month ago, when she made the reservations for this trip. She really wanted Bene to tell you himself, you see.'

'Is that so?'

'I've never met him, but apparently he is really something. A kind of magnetic personality that brings everyone around to his side. You know how some people are?'

'I see.' He sits up and runs his thumb over the corner of the photograph of the teenage boy. His own hands are dark with the sun, wrinkled at the knuckles. The nails are scraggy and bitten down. The boy, so unlike him, seems flawless and unmarked by the world. What could he possibly have to say?

Bene would be a different kind of man altogether than him, who works with his hands. Kojo leads teams of people who know things about the soil, the disease vectors, and how to negotiate in conflict zones. How could a boy understand any of that?

# Sixteen

## Lena

### Flying into Geneina, Darfur, October 2003

There were more military personnel and police in the Khartoum airport this time. More people too, skittish and unpredictable. The planes were not announced ahead of time. When they came in, people walked with tense shoulders as if they would prefer to run, but didn't want to draw attention to themselves.

She had enough experience to know to never take out her cameras at an airport. Especially not one that is dual use, shared with the air force. You couldn't miss the lines of newly arrived planes in the military section. Some were painted in desert camouflage, others were white with the names of companies or countries, written in Arabic or Russian with the occasional English. There was movement and money pouring into this new war in the west, alliances being made.

That lesson about military planes was from an old journalist friend, Stefan. He was a brilliant photographer. His work was in black and white, printed in *The Sunday Times, The New York Times, Le Monde,* AFP, the

UN's news wires, and all over the world. When he visited Angola, he brought some copies of his award-winning articles with him, folded and fraying at the edges. He had shot photos in all the big crises of the 80s and 90s: Ethiopia's famine, the civil war in Lebanon, the Balkan wars, South Africa's elections, and the Rwandan genocide. His most famous photos were graphic images from 1994 Kigali. Kojo introduced Lena to him when Stefan was doing a photo-essay for *Time* about disabled survivors of land-mines in Angola.

Stefan was a tall, gangly man. He had dull green eyes, the colour of army fatigues, and always wore his blonde-grey hair in a mess. Perhaps Kojo thought that Stefan could give Lena a sense of how to sustain yourself in the business of photographing humanitarian situations.

However, Stefan killed himself not long after.

It didn't happen immediately. It seemed that it took years for the impact of witnessing genocide and other horrific world events to sink in. He left the field, went home to Paris and overdosed on heroin. It would have been assumed to be an accident, except he'd left a note talking about Rwanda.

Lena had heard about it through other journalists that she knew. She remembered the note ended with the phrase: 'No more nightmares.'

She was starting to understand that feeling, of having lived through something intense, and carrying that intensity around with you. Whether you wanted to shake it off or not, it clung to you and changed your perspective on everything.

Landing in Geneina felt right this time, as Lena was greeted by newly recruited CWW staff. Even though she didn't know them personally, they were part of the same team. Most of them were Sudanese staff who had worked in the war in the south, recently rotated out to Darfur. They were kind to her and generous with sharing their expertise, but kept a certain distance. She would have to prove her usefulness in order to earn their friendship and respect. It was a satisfying feeling, knowing that her earlier efforts at assessment led to the establishment of new CWW bases and programmes, which were just taking root.

When she saw who was driving her home from the airport, Lena didn't hesitate to wrap her arms around the neck of her dear old friend with the magenta hair.

'You accepted the post!' she said to Jeanette. 'What about Angola? Where's Brad?'

Her friend swatted away the many questions and bundled her into the car.

'Angola's changed. The work has changed. They don't need field nurses anymore. They need people distributing World Bank money, building hospitals and roads. That's not me. I'm good in the field. One-on-one, with the mothers and the babies and the sick old guys. I'm not a bureaucrat. Kojo mentioned this post as a three-month position, for a change.' She gestured around her.

Lena looked through the windscreen at the landscape, wondering what Jeanette thought when she first saw it. Although they had both been in the dry highlands of Angola, Darfur felt a world apart. The horizon stretched out in front of them, unbroken except for small settlements built in concrete blocks tinted the same colour as the sand. Compounds were clustered around occasional oases, buildings at angles to each other to provide as much shade as possible for the inhabitants. In the inner courtyards, she knew that occasionally there would be secret gardens of dates and flowers, carefully tended with borrowed water. From the outside, signs of life were hidden.

The Sahel desert was never far away. The dryness in the air sucked all the moisture out of your skin and left you feeling raw and exposed. It made you want to lick your lips, even though you knew you would only get salt. She bit down to try to stop the impulse. She tasted sand already, even before spending any time in the elements.

They arrived at a guest house that was also functioning as the CWW office. 'Brad is thinking about coming too, for the logistics post,' Jeanette said. 'But as an American it's much harder to get the working visa, especially now that the US has imposed sanctions on the government.'

'I didn't think you'd want to go anywhere without him,' Lena said, then wished she hadn't.

'You know, I'm passionate about that bloke. Always have been. But it's hard to find posts for two people who are together, but who aren't married.' Jeanette had been married – and divorced – before she came to the field, and swore she could not go through that again.

'And this isn't post-war Angola,' Jeanette said, shifting into Lena's professional briefing. 'I know I don't have to tell you the history and background; you did a great job scouting out operations before the logisticians came in. It made my work so much easier after your networking with the medical NGOs and their logisticians. But some things have changed in the past few months. There's huge and growing humanitarian need here, but not a lot of agencies. And it's getting more and more difficult to operate.'

Inside the compound, she brought Lena into a room with no windows. 'This is our safe room. If there's ever any threat against staff or an attack on the compound, people congregate here and call SOS Air Ambulance. You know the number?'

'Memorised it.'

'Good. There are some flares that you can use from the rooftop to signal where you are. There's the interior staircase to get up there. And this is the sat phone that never leaves this compound, *never*, unless it goes with the last person standing, who might be me. Until someone more senior comes.' Jeanette looked at Lena's face. 'Do you know if Kojo is planning to come out for a visit?'

'I don't know,' Lena said. 'He has a lot of responsibilities, now that HQ decided to restructure and merge all CWW's Africa regions into one. He's in Senegal at the moment.'

'Trying to speak French?'

'Probably... You know him. He always wants people to feel he's making an effort.'

'He's got good intuition,' Jeanette said. 'Makes him a shrewd leader. But he takes his time, too much time, with some decisions that would come easier to other people. I feel the need to shake him, sometimes.'

'Oh, he's his own man,' Lena said, acutely aware that they both knew their boss was also her lover. 'I can't convince him to do anything that wouldn't come naturally. We rarely talk, these weeks when we're both travelling.'

# Kojo

### Isle de Gorée, off the coast of Dakar, Senegal, October 2003

The short ferry ride cleared his mind and left him ready for the staff meeting. He was gearing up to lead a three-day CWW conference about the strategic direction of the organisation in Africa. He would take on the role of the steady, cheerful, approachable NGO leader once they got in the conference room. He had prepared an inspiring opening speech, strategic plans setting a confident way forward, jokes in the coffee breaks and soothing words to the select board members who had made the trip out from Europe and America. He would do all that, with the effort it demanded. But not just yet.

He loved being back on the West African coast. It reminded him of holidays in Ghana as a child. He had grown up inland, and for him the coast meant something fresh and different. He both belonged there and didn't belong. It made him a bit giddy; he wanted to find a reason to laugh, even at nothing.

He stood away from his colleagues, taking a break from the professional banter, and felt the breeze on his face. What was it about the ocean air that always made him feel young? Maybe because he saw the sea so rarely, it rubbed some of the years off him. He ran his hands over his two-day stubble.

The boat arrived and people stumbled off. Some were tourists, looking up and around at the pastel-drenched walls and 18th-century alleyways. Others acted like worried commuters, head down, preparing for the tasks or confrontations that lay ahead. He wondered which category he belonged to. Both probably, or neither.

As a West African, he often felt his way between edges. That he should be able to fit in anywhere in the region was assumed, but he wasn't quite chameleon enough. He didn't speak French very well, despite years of trying. His Arabic wasn't great either. But he'd travelled enough to know that there was something about being from West Africa that made him malleable. He could bend according to the tasks and context. He wouldn't have to change, not too much. Subtle shifts, dictated by the needs of the situation, nothing more.

He separated from the crowd and wandered into the sandstone-brick alleys. The colours were bleached by the day, the shadows growing with the late afternoon descent of the sun. Even the shutters with their bright blues felt quieter as the light diminished. He liked the narrowing feeling of the different alleys. After a few turns he found that he could reach both walls with arms outstretched. It gave him a sense of protection. There were doorways to duck into if needed. He felt you could contemplate there. Scattered thoughts could come to calm.

The narrow alleyway hit a T-junction that glowed with a warm red hue. He walked around a corner and emerged to see the approaching sunset throwing soft light onto *La Maison des Esclaves*.

The pink paint, dusted with sprayed sand from recent storms, made this monument to slavery seem too beautiful. They shouldn't have made it look like a work of art. Slavery didn't need that. The truth of the matter was brutal and dirty and the worst of humanity. He opposed this polishing of the truth to make it appeal. He didn't go in. He didn't need to walk through the door of no return. He knew there would be nothing but ocean below, and the place was haunted by the voices of people forced on the sea journey to slavery.

He missed Lena. He wanted her there with him; to hold his hand and to rub her thumb along his knuckles. Would she agree with him about the monument? Maybe, maybe not. She had some strong views about art and representation. He couldn't predict what would spark her interest or her scorn. He was still learning about her. But she also had a quiet respect for his experience, and that of others. While she could document and listen and observe, she knew which stories were hers to tell, and which ones she had to support. She treaded lightly, careful not to trample.

It was nice to have a break from Nairobi. It was a tough city at times. In some neighbourhoods and corners, you knew what to expect and braced yourself for it. But the crime had reached further out, and the threats flickered in the margins of his mind every day. There was a low-level but constant fear of car-jackings, violent theft, or something happening to his team and the people he cared about.

He gave Lena lectures about being street-smart and cautious. But he had to admit that he was nearly as much of an outsider as she was. He stood out from the Kenyans by way of his accent and face shape and a whole host of other small details. As an ex-pat, he could easily be preyed upon by criminals, and had to keep his attention focused most of the time: during the commute, and at key moments like when he opened the gate in the morning or pulled the car into the garage at night. It was important to be clear when there was a change in staffing, to know who the new guards were, and whether there were any grievances or debts he should hear about. It was exhausting.

In some ways it was not that different from Malanje, except that in a city like Nairobi you could never say you knew all the key characters, understood their alliances and motivations. Even though there was not an actual war around you, it felt like a potential one was rumbling just beneath the surface.

Maybe he and Lena needed some R&R together. To take a break somewhere calm, somewhere like here, Isle de Gorée, before her next mission. When she got back from Darfur, she'd need something. To spend time together and talk, really talk. Make love in the morning with the blinds closed against the sun, emerge by noon. No deadlines or staff meetings or emails to write. Leave the CWW mobile phone to somebody else to mind for a week.

They'd never done it that way. They'd met on the job, fallen in love on the job. Survived threats, sealed their bond, all on the job. Sometimes he wondered if she would love him, if it wasn't for the work they shared. She would, wouldn't she? Would he love her? Not a question. But if it wasn't for humanitarian work, what would they have in common?

He left the monument and walked along the shore. The sun was right on the horizon and would soon dip below the surface. The water was calm, and the fishermen were in. Their boats were slim and shaped like the fingers of the palm fronds washed in by the waves. Now hauled up on the sand, they were in a line, colourful and personalised. Some had freshly painted designs of sea creatures, abstract shapes, or things he couldn't recognise. Others were branded with people's names, sayings in French or Wolof. He wished he was better with languages.

Some were painted with lines from the Bible, he knew that much. Others were quotes from the Qur'an, perhaps. It seemed like poetry, in any case. Maybe words for good luck at sea. A good catch, favourable winds. He wondered if the writing brought the luck it promised.

He stopped and sat down. He took his feet out of his shoes and socks and dug them under the cool sand. He would have to brush them off and freshen up later to play the part of CWW Africa director. But not just yet.

A group of young boys were playing around the fishing boats. They hid and dipped down, giggling and whispering. They brought their heads up briefly, one at a time, taking turns spying on him.

His skin was the same colour as theirs – was it so clear that he was an outsider? He looked down at his button-down shirt, pressed this morning. The khakis that he always wore on airplanes. The polished leather shoes next to him with the socks neatly stowed inside. These boys were in flip-flops and torn shorts, happily playing in the breeze in the last minutes of afternoon sun. No, he would always be a stranger to them.

# Seventeen

## Lena

### Geneina, Darfur, December 2003

The rainy season should have been over, that's what everyone said. And it was, in relation to any raindrops hitting the ground. The shallow desert rivers were swollen to their heights and the water was quickly disappearing back into the earth. But the storm clouds remained. The local staff said they had never seen anything like it. Scowling over the flat horizon, these sculpted columns rose up, threatening the mortals below. The effect was thunder and cloud-to-cloud lightning, but no rain. It was eerie, like someone playing with fire but not quite letting it roar.

Lena was on the rooftop of the CWW compound. The flat concrete roof had raised edges all around, so she was protected from the sight of passers by. Painted white to reflect the sun, it rumbled with the air conditioner and the generator. She rested with her back against the stand for the water tank, sheltered by its shadow. Even though the sun was falling in the sky, it would still be horribly hot until proper sunset.

She was going over her handwritten notes from the past few days visiting camps with new arrivals from North Darfur. She was looking for meaning in the stories, some pattern or clue. Anything to help her interpret what was going on. She read again and reorganised the names of people's villages, looking for possible explanations of these movements of people. Was there an advantage for the Janjaweed to attack this village rather than that one? What was important about that area? She unfolded a geological map that also showed elevations, rivers and traditional trade routes. Was that going to be a military installation, the corridor they were ushering people away from? How about that field – a landing strip?

She looked for reasons why people were being forced to move. She tried to remain dispassionate, like a journalist seeking facts for the record, rather than a woman interacting with these people face to face. That seemed the professional thing to do.

She had interviewed women, families, teenagers. Not very many men, that was always the way – most were in hiding, in exile or joining the grow-ing rebellion. There were girls who had been raped and became mothers at fourteen or fifteen years old. Grandmothers looking after their daughter's children after complications. Sisters desperate to hear what had happened to their older brothers who had gone out to look after the animals and never returned to the family compound.

Lena listened and took copious notes. She also took some pictures, but respected people's reluctance to provide photographic evidence. She tried not to absorb their emotions too much. Terror, despair, and paralysing sadness took over these people, and she couldn't let that seep into her mind. Her notebook pages were running out and she started writing in each line twice, to cram in all the information as the stories kept coming. She felt that she owed them this: testimony, preserved.

Many reported they had been forced to leave their homes without warn-ing. The stories were familiar and yet precise enough to ring true. Lots of people were looking for missing boys, aged between eleven and twenty. Hope had left their mothers' eyes already. You knew what happened to boys of that age. Either they were sucked into the rebel ranks, or executed by the army. For the lucky ones, you heard reports that they banded together to walk longer distances, to safe places across the border, in Kenya or Ethiopia. The great distances from western Sudan made that unlikely, but there were still wisps of hope.

And the Janjaweed – the horseback men. People shuddered when they spoke of them. The idea of the Janjaweed scared people more than the bombings, for some reason. Their hoofbeats were heard from miles away. The dust clouds rose on the horizon even before you could make out the silhouettes of the individual mercenaries. Their scarves wrapped around their faces left just slits for their eyes, hiding all individual identity. They didn't seem human, more of an extension of some malevolent beast.

Their words, when they shouted, were unintelligible, people said. They were from countries distant and alien. But the meaning was clear. They only went to certain villages, where the rebel groups and their families were rumoured to be based. Their horses' hooves trampled on children. They kicked over clean water stands and poured petrol over food stores to set them alight. They never gave a reason for the attacks. Or a warning. There was no room to negotiate, as the elders had done in the past. There was just the sound of the hooves, coming to destroy village after village. Life after life.

She looked over her notes, dozens upon dozens of interviews so far. All pointing in one direction of indiscriminate harm to villagers, based on their ethnicity. Her hand shook a little as she wrote down her conclusions.

And who was she to say? Just a photographer from London with less than two years of field experience in other contexts. No training in international humanitarian law or human rights. Just the power of observation and the things she'd learned from colleagues over the last year and a half. It was minimal. She wasn't an authority on warfare.

But she couldn't deny it. People here were reporting being corralled into camps by these ghostly horse-riding creatures. The camps had little food or water. People were starving and humanitarian aid was being restricted. The only explanation they believed was that this was being done under the orders of the government in Khartoum.

And they were terrified.


'He can't say that, not the G-word,' Jeanette argued with her over dinner that night.

'He's the head of the UN here, can't he just say it as it is?'

'Oh darling, you don't understand a thing about this government, do you? They hate the UN. Blame it for prolonging the war in the south, for whatever that opinion's worth. For getting in the way with them finishing the job. They could throw the UN out at a moment's notice and then where would we be? The humanitarian community, the patchwork we try to pull together, would be leaderless, like a headless chicken. And now that the Darfurian rebels have given the army a bloody nose, the government won't listen to anyone.'

'But these are violations of human rights on a huge scale! This could be evidence of war crimes!'

Jeanette put down her fork and studied Lena's face. 'Honey, I think you're getting carried away. We're not the experts. It's not CWW's job to say whether it is war crimes or not. We're not international lawyers. We don't have that kind of forensic-evidence-gathering capacity.'

'But it's everyone's responsibility, is it not? To say something if there is a risk of another genocide? What does "never again" mean, if not that?'

'I don't know what it means. Maybe it doesn't mean anything, if people aren't willing to enforce it.'

Lena couldn't believe what she was hearing. This, from a woman of compassion? 'That's a terrible thing to say.'

'I know darling.' Jeanette's eyes softened as she considered her words. 'I'm not a monster, love. But I know these forces are much bigger than you, bigger than me. Than CWW. Than even the UN, unfortunately. What can we do? We're just here a short time, and we try to save lives by preventing cholera in these camps and treating malaria and malnutrition, and maybe that's good enough.'

'Good enough? You think that's enough?'

'I only have my own two hands, Lena. And God gave me the knowledge and motivation to be a nurse, so that's what I'm doing.'

'And what if it was Rwanda all over again, like 1994? What would you do?'

'I haven't the faintest idea what I'd do. Get the hell out, I imagine. And live with nightmares and PTSD for the rest of my life.'

Lena didn't answer. She thought back to what Petra had said, the last visit to Darfur. If you are only one pace ahead of the shadows, what happens when they threaten to overtake?

# Part III

# Eighteen

## Kojo

**Nairobi, 22 June 2022**

He drives back to the house after his unsuccessful airport trip. His office mobile is ringing, but he shuts it off. He just needs some time to think.

The guard seems startled to see him. It is possible he was sleeping in the guard booth. How he could sleep in that tiny shack is hard to believe, but Kojo supposes that if he slumped his head over his forearms, then slept standing up, it could be done. If you were more than exhausted. No matter – it was the middle of the morning. Not a likely time for criminality or planned abductions.

Kojo turns off the ignition and sits in the car for a moment. He is out of breath. He puts his fingers to the inside of his wrist. The pulse is a bit high. Probably the airport coffee. It is famous for stewing all night, selling the worst of the bottom of the barrel to the poor souls waiting outside international arrivals.

What is he waiting for? Inside the house he will probably see Paradisa, and have to explain what he was doing away from the office. Or maybe this is the day for her prayer meeting? He can't remember.

He never comes home during the daytime unexplained. Just that one time when he fell ill. That was the only time, soon after she and Omondi moved in.


Dengue fever. What a terrible disease. The doctor thought he'd caught it in the refugee camps in Gulu in Uganda, but he'll never be sure. He had held a bit of African arrogance before that. He saw the muzungus fall ill their first season in the field, and he'd thought that he was stronger than that. He'd grown up in Africa, what could go wrong? He'd had all his jabs and the medical care with CWW was good. He took his anti-malarials when he needed to. But no one had predicted the dengue outbreak, so there was little warning.

That awful fever. The feeling like his joints were all being pulled apart, all of them, at the same time. To bend them felt excruciating, and yet to move was necessary. The fever made you mad to move from the pain. You couldn't stay still, you just kept writhing and twisting, sweating and screaming out to anyone to make it stop. Paradisa had stayed with him then. She didn't have to, Lord knows it must've been difficult. But she was there. Let in the doctors from the private medical practice. Arranged for the expensive house calls. Learned how to do the injections and to change the IV fluids.

Did he ask her to be by his bedside? Or did he just assume, that because she was there, she would stay? She was well paid, of course. And dengue isn't contagious through human contact, so she and Omondi were not in any danger. But there was always a feeling that she had agreed willingly. She wasn't the type to walk away when things became unsavoury or too difficult. And when the fever and sweats washed away, and the pain subsided, he was left with the feeling that he was only a residue of the man he once was. The container, the skin was intact but the substance inside was weakened and drained.

He remembers opening his eyes. She was next to him, reading a magazine about hairstyles that she liked, one that she'd read many times before. When she saw that he was awake, he was going to speak but she shushed him and put down the magazine. She shifted the pillows behind him so he could sit up to drink from a fresh glass of water.

She smelled of fresh shampoo and something else he couldn't name. He wondered what he smelled like, after days of sweating and not brushing his teeth. He ran his tongue over the enamel and they felt sandy and neglected. He accepted the water with a nod of thanks and held it in both hands. The pain was a bit less but still lingering like a sad memory. He liked the cool smoothness of the glass, rolled it back and forth, although he was afraid he might drop it. He pressed it to his cheek. It was such a contrast that he gasped.

'You had us worried there, Mr Appiah,' she said, pulling up the sheet to cover him again. He tried to ask her not to trouble with it, but she waved his words away. He drank hungrily but suddenly felt like he could not drink any more or he might vomit. His hand started to fall, and she caught it, before the glass slipped.

'You just need some rest now,' she said. She picked up her magazine as if to go.

He wanted her to stay, but couldn't find the words. His bones ached like they'd been beaten but not quite broken. It became just too painful to have his eyes open, and he didn't have any fight left.

He heard her move to the door, and pause.

'Mr Appiah?'

'Yes?'

'Who's Lena? You were calling for her while you were in the fever. Shall I contact someone for you, sir?'

He was too tired to shake his head. 'She's no one,' he said in a whisper. 'No one now.'

# Nineteen

## Lena

**Geneina, December 2003**

The woman shifted and played with the fabric draped over her legs. It was worn thin and colourless, but it still provided some dignity. She was struggling to explain what she'd been through, and the interpreter wasn't helping.

Lena appreciated that it was getting late in the day, and curfew was soon. They were not allowed on the roads within an hour of sunset. You never knew when the Janjaweed were going to launch their next night-time raid. Well, some people seemed to know. The local government officials were extremely polite but shared little. Whenever they radioed to say that they could not, unfortunately, guarantee security on a certain road at a certain time, you knew you had to get back to base.

Lena squatted down to put herself at the same level as the woman. The interpreter, Wadood, was a bit too haughty, she noted in her head. It didn't make sense to be standing tall when this woman was sharing such personal information. Next time she would try to get a female interpreter. You had to recognise that these interviews were extremely sensitive.

The woman, whose name was Aarya, drew a circle around her own bony knee, through the fabric. Again and again, this circle of the forefinger. She did not look at Lena's face, just down at this circling. Perhaps it was soothing. Or something to occupy the mind instead of going into someplace more difficult.

Lena tried to bring Aarya back to the thread of her story. There were frequent breaks where the woman seemed to struggle. She would shake her head and twitch suddenly to the side, as if something had burned her. Lena wondered if she was feeling feverish, or was psychologically damaged by the trauma, or both.

The story so far was not unusual. The woman reported that she was from Farchana village and lived there with her husband and six children. When the Janjaweed came, they had no warning. There was the thumping of hooves in the distance, not even enough time to prepare any food or belongings. She swept up her youngest, who was still breastfeeding, in a cloth on her back and ran with two of her young children.

Her husband ran as well, but he must have gone in another direction because they lost contact. She had not seen or heard from him since. This was three months ago. She had no news of her older children, and worried that the eldest boy may have been captured.

'You know what happens when they capture the boys,' Wadood, the interpreter, said.

'Is that what she said?' Lena didn't look up from the woman, although she aimed the question to him.

'She doesn't have to say it,' he said. 'Everyone knows.'

'What is she actually saying?' Lena said, annoyed. 'I'd like to know how she's choosing to express it.'

'She's not really saying anything,' he said, and Lena had to admit he was right. The interview had descended into mumbles that Wadood didn't bother to translate. The woman wouldn't meet anyone's eyes while she circled her knee non-stop.

'I think she's traumatised,' Lena said. 'We should stop. Please tell her I'd like to thank her for telling us her story.' She waited while he translated. She hoped he was choosing a kind and respectful phrasing. 'And that I think she is really brave. And that her children are lucky to have her, as a parent. To protect them.'

When the interpreter said the last words, the woman smiled a weak smile and looked at Lena. It seemed like she wanted to ask a question herself, but lacked the courage to try.

'Should we do one more interview?' Lena asked.

'Is that wise?' Wadood said, looking at his watch. 'Don't you have what you need?'

'Maybe that other lady, isn't she Aarya's sister?'

'Oh, alright. One last one.'

'Thanks Wadood. You're the best.' She didn't mean a word of it, but had to keep things civil.

They found her sister Hiba, and she was willing to speak. She came from the same village and had also fled the Janjaweed attack. She was much more outspoken than her sister, and demanded some answers. She raised her voice and went on at length in her local language, looking straight at Lena, standing with her hands on her hips.

Hiba asked why they were left with no protection, the translator recounted. The Janjaweed, she said, they don't come out of the air. Someone is paying their rations. She was shouting now. Someone is paying for their boots! Someone is feeding them and their horses! What is the UN going to do about it?

Lena tried to formulate a response, knowing nothing would satisfy this woman. She was not the UN, not a peacekeeper, she explained. She was not authorised to gather legal evidence for crimes, although she possibly could. She was just a communications officer from a medium-sized water-and-sanitation NGO. But she promised the woman that she would listen to whatever she wanted to say, and that she would make sure the facts were raised in Khartoum, Nairobi, Geneva and Brussels, where CWW had offices. She would take the story to the media, if that was what this woman wanted.

Hiba started again before Lena's thin promises were finished. She raised her voice and punctuated her story with sound effects of muffled screams and yells. Lena tried not to grimace as she waited for the interpretation.

'She says her sister was held down and attacked by four men,' Wadood said. 'The only reason Hiba wasn't also set upon was because she kept shouting so loudly they didn't want to do it, and kicked her in the stomach instead until she fainted. She says the Janjaweed aren't ghosts. They are men, powerful men. And they are doing evil, on a large scale.'

'Why are they doing it?' Lena asked.

Wadood raised a pathetic smile, as if he wished he didn't have to ask such a stupid question. But he duly translated. And then when Hiba answered, he turned back to Lena with a 'told-you-so' look.

'Because they can,' he said simply. 'No one stops them.'

Hiba was clearly frustrated with Lena and waved away her questions. She would say no more. She spat in the dust and walked away.


Her last night in Geneina, Lena went back on the rooftop with Jeanette. The air was clear, although a sandstorm was rumoured to be rolling across the land in the coming days. The flat landscape provided clear views on all sides for miles. The sunset had come and gone, leaving the sky a dull orange fading to dark grey.

Lena sipped from her water bottle, which had the reassuring taste of iodine to ensure that no bacteria would survive. She ran her hands over her shoulders to hold back a shiver as the heat disappeared from the day.

She heard them before she saw them, a rumble coming closer. Then, in the last vestiges of daylight, her eyes made out the outlines of men on horseback in the distance. There seemed to be hundreds of them, but their silhouettes overlapped and merged, moving so fast as a group it was impossible to tell. Their gallops beat out a scattered rhythm, not uniform. It was chaotic but steady all the same, providing just scant warning to the villages in their path.

With horror, Lena realised that they were heading straight towards the refugee camp she had been in earlier that day, with Wadood, Aarya, Hiba and all the others. The Janjaweed were beating their way across a flat and barren landscape to an unprotected settlement of war-worn women and children. There was no reason to be going there, just to cause terror. There would be no negotiations, and no mercy.

There was no time to warn them; Lena knew no radios or satellite phones were kept in the camp overnight. Jeanette ran down to the SOS room to try to get the word out through the UN in Geneina and Khartoum, to see if anything could be done.

Lena was powerless to help. From the rooftop, she saw torches light up when the horsemen reached the edges of the camp protected only by a thorny wood border fence. The refugees could not get out, nor hide. Horses reared up to kick down the barrier, and then many galloped inside. Even with the distance, Lena could sense the fear. Fire leapt up around the fencing and flashed from inside the camp. The flimsy tents and makeshift shelters would be no resistance against determined malice.

In what proved to be a few minutes, but felt achingly long, the Janjaweed on horseback started jumping back over the fencing and leaving the burning camp behind. Mission accomplished. Punishment inflicted, the motivation for it to be dissected by peacekeepers and journalists later. They would study the ashes and scratch their heads. What was the possible reason behind the violence? Why this refugee camp, and not others? What purpose could indiscriminate violence serve?

Jeanette came back upstairs and put her arm around Lena. They were both shivering and could not look away. They said nothing; no more could be done. Everything that made sense had already been said, reported to headquarters and the UN. What lingered was a feeling of helplessness and rage with nowhere to go.

Lena later asked herself why she did not try to take any photographs. But with the distance and the nightfall, and the limited range of her lenses, it wouldn't have translated into useful information for anyone who hadn't been there. It wouldn't have been good for evidence either. Even if she had taken photographs, they would have been too late to save lives.

Is this how Stefan had felt? She thought about him, her old photographer friend who had killed himself. Thought about him more and more, when she was in Darfur.

# Twenty

## Kojo

### Flight to Paris, 22 June 2022

This isn't like him, this spontaneous trip. He knows Jeanette is surprised, but she shouldn't be. She's known him for so long, how could she have thought that this secret wouldn't affect him? He isn't known for fast decisions, but it just seems like this moment holds something important that has eluded him all his life.

Once Jeanette heard from Lena that Bene was hurt and in hospital, Kojo had to go to Paris. He didn't end up speaking to Lena, and to be honest, he still isn't ready to. He has so many feelings tangled up inside, feelings he isn't used to. Like fury. And resentment. And a desire to get back at her, like revenge. It doesn't feel nice, not at all. He is usually very comfortable with his sense of self as a calm, contemplative man. No need for anger, that shows a lack of control. He is balanced and sensible. He is intelligent, savvy in his work negotiations, and has built a career to be proud of. He's worked hard for that.

And he's made his peace with his domestic situation. He doesn't know if Paradisa is going to stay with him in the long term, but he has the feeling she will. He will take pleasure in helping to raise Omondi. To show him how to be a man, how to study hard, how to figure out what God has put him on earth to do. He thinks Omondi might be a good lawyer. Probably not an engineer; the boy doesn't take to tools and building like the others. But that's okay. Maybe he will be a professor. He has some deep intelligence in him.

You need to accept children as they are. Observe them closely, nurture them as they make their own decisions, and then you stand back. At least that's what he thinks you do. They have to be able to make mistakes and learn about themselves. Know thyself – isn't that the most important lesson of all?

And yet here he is, impulsively on a flight to a city he doesn't know. Where they speak a language he doesn't speak, to find a boy who is ostensibly his son, but they've never met. He's never had the chance to hold him, observe him, learn about him, teach him. He's been absent these seventeen years, and now this young man has nearly got himself killed. Over what? Sounds like it's over a girl. A French girl he can't have known very long.

Kojo would laugh if it wasn't so serious. How typical of a teenager. Getting yourself in trouble over a girl at a moment's notice. He could remember feeling that way, once. Love so powerful it dominated thoughts like an obsession.

But he is a grown man now. He has grey in his stubble and has been bald for decades. People look up to him. They expect him back in the office, and will be puzzled at the sudden absence. These people have substituted for family over the years, as it slowly became clear that there was no one else.

How is he going to explain this to them? To anybody?

It was soon after Lena had left, March, 2004. No, April. He was still trying to piece it together, her sudden irrational flight. He should have taken time off, that was clear later. His skin was dry and irritated – he remembers that. No matter how much cocoa butter he used, the eczema always came back in times of high stress. He tried to hide his painfully cracked knuckles and bleeding wrists under his pressed shirts. Cufflinks were carefully selected to be of the right material. The cheaper ones, made of nickel or lead, would set his skin off. Better to go with gold or silver. But you never knew what might be under a thin layer of paint.

He needed to look the part for this occasion. He was invited by the Rwandan government to attend an official visit to commemorate the ten-year anniversary of the Rwandan genocide. It was an honour for CWW to be invited as part of the international events. Elite organisations and leaders from the UN and around the world were invited by the government to show respect for what they had been through, and conquered.

He was there with the Ghanaian ambassador to Rwanda, a man named John Kanda whom he had known in school in the Volta region. John had done very well for himself, and always remembered his early connections. He remained in close touch with the Accra elite, and never failed to drop in a word about Kojo's brother, Kumi. This time he was saying that Kumi had been elected the representative of Ashanti businessmen in Accra's South District, a very prestigious position. John never seemed to tire of the advantage of knowing more about Kojo's family than he did. Kojo had to be polite, so he smiled in a way that he hoped translated as yes, he knew the story. But no, he didn't need to hear more.

The occasion didn't call for much talking. It was a solemn and quiet affair. The official press photographers took photos from a respectful distance, and there was no hum of interviews or celebrities. No dancing, no music. Helicopters overhead beat their propellers, but were just there as a precaution, the ambassador said. Precaution against what, it wasn't clear.

There didn't seem any risk of violence or riot. The palpable risk remained one of forgetting the events of the past. The ceremony was an elaborate piece of theatre played out in front of an international audience to assure them that never again would they live through such a tragedy.

The president of Rwanda made a speech, but Kojo was sitting so far back he could not make out the words. The meaning was clear enough. Never again. Repeated in English, French, and Kinyarwanda. He learned the phrase by heart.

A full army regiment of over five hundred men stood in formation on the hillsides on either side of the speaker's podium. As the speeches continued to flow, Kojo watched these men. They were perfectly still, in uniforms that looked of the highest quality. Total discipline, and total confidence from being part of the formation. The government, the army and the society would ensure that genocide would never happen again here. Over 800,000 innocent people were slaughtered at an astonishing rate, in under a hundred days. The fastest rate of killing ever recorded. Impossible to imagine.

In 1994, where was he? In Lokichogio, working for the UN's Operation Lifeline Sudan – airlifts to prevent mass starvation in the south. He hardly thought about that anymore. They had really believed they were providing a lifeline to Sudanese displaced peoples and Ethiopians on the brink of starvation because of the war. It was a very tough situation, but he never felt like it was something intentional, not like the genocidaires in Rwanda. The situation inside Sudan was grim, and yes, the rebels and the Sudanese government both manipulated the reports and supplies to their advantage. But there was a general feeling that, somehow, the UN's agreement would hold, and prevent mass deaths. There wasn't some orchestrated plan, or so they chose to believe.

He remembers hearing about Rwanda on the BBC World Service, but he shook his head at the time. Everyone had thought that the reports couldn't have been true. And then, as the news dripped out and then came flooding through, the extent of the horrors became known.

He had friends who had been there, at the time of the genocide. Colleagues who'd rotated out of Loki, then met up again in Angola on the other side of the continent. That happened with people serving in humanitarian operations. The journalists, they were who he remembers most. They had a damaged look about them. Hell, many humanitarian workers bore that look, and anaesthetised themselves with drinking or sex or both. But there was something about the journalists. Or maybe he just remembered them later, once he knew Lena. Those people who tried to document the crimes while they unfolded. They were the first ones in to make the early reports. He thought of Stefan, that photographer friend he introduced to Lena. He remembers the look on her face when they learned that Stefan had killed himself. She didn't talk about it, but her expression was a complicated tangle of emotions. As if she both understood and couldn't understand that level of despair.

Kojo wished that Lena was there with him, at this memorial. Not taking photos. Just with him, holding his hand. She would understand about the eczema, would take care with his cufflinks. She wouldn't need to work to serve a deadline. She would just be there, with him. Just be. Together.

It had been two months since she had left him. How old would she have been in 1994? Just a teenager, no doubt. Taking her photographs in South London, knowing nothing about the wider world. Or maybe a little. She always said he didn't give her enough credit. Didn't she say that? Or maybe he'd imagined it.

Where was she? He needed her there, but she had left him. That was the truth of the matter. Extended R&R was the explanation, and he was left to fill in the blanks. Maybe she hadn't been happy. Maybe he hadn't been listening closely enough. Those last two missions to Darfur in close succession, she was working too hard. She was jumpy, and touchy at small suggestions. He never should have let her burn out like that.

The speeches finished. Everyone was invited to join the queue and enter the new genocide memorial. There were coffins made out of stone, stacked five high, as you walked up the slope. Stained glass lined the entrance. He didn't want to walk into the place; it felt like a tomb. But he was with the ambassador and all the others, and it was expected. Anything else would upset the flow of people.

The photographs inside were graphic, but not unexpected. They were close up and brutal. Some that were censored ten years ago were now on display, showing crushed skeletons and dismembered body parts. Children's belongings, sets of teeth, and confiscated weapons were all presented as evidence – catalogued and categorised. Videos on repeat had the words of survivors talking about rape, imprisonment, arson, losing friends and family. Having to fake death to stay alive.

It was too much. Even though he'd worked in some of the last decade's worst humanitarian crises, he couldn't comprehend this level of brutality. No museum, no video was going to help him understand the *why*. Why did this happen, to these people, at this time? Why did no one intervene to prevent it?

Some people would want to narrow the blame down to a particular group of people or a certain type, but he was not so sure. Other people turn to God for answers or consolation. Or turn away from God, when no satisfactory response is forthcoming.

He couldn't absorb any more of the scene in front of him, and kept thinking about Lena. When he emerged out of the building he looked over his shoulder, hoping to see her face. There were many Europeans there, but none that had her look: long black hair, usually in a plait or a bun, tall with defined cheekbones; it was a face that didn't look like it wanted to smile when she was resting or thinking.

What would she think of this museum? He had the feeling she might hate it, but then again, he could not read her mind.

She was not there. She was nowhere near him now. Where should he turn? He didn't have anybody. Without Lena there, he had lost his compass. Even when they had disagreed, the talks with her helped him make his decisions and judgements. Plot a way forward. Whatever they faced. It made more sense, when she was there with him. Without her, he was completely at sea.

# Twenty-one

## Lena

### Dover, England, 22 June 2022

What a mess, this day of all days, to have a rail strike. Lena can't believe how complicated this has become. Her stomach is gurgling with too much coffee, sloshing with acidity. She hopes the driver can't hear.

She is in the cab of a lorry with a man she just met, waiting in the queue at the café by the barriers at the port. She couldn't get on a Eurostar train to cross the Channel, so she caught a coach from Victoria and tried to get on the ferry to Calais. But the ferry was completely full, even for walk-ons with no baggage. She couldn't believe it. Still, a desperate mother in search of a solution is never deterred for long. She started talking with strangers at the coffee shop and sure enough, sympathy ensued for her cause. Now, just a few hours after receiving the news about Bene, she hopes that she will soon cross the water to reach France.

The cab smells of tobacco and cheese and onion crisps. The driver, Bill, is a very big white man. He fills up his side of the bench seat with a wide belly, and his cap nearly touches the roof. He wears a checked short-sleeved shirt that looks recently pressed, with red braces to keep his trousers in place. He slaps his belly apologetically and explains that a belt is out of the question, except a seatbelt of course.

'My wife bought me these.' He snaps one of the braces at his shoulder. 'Said I should always try to look respectable. Bought a set of twelve, all colours.'

Lena likes the idea of someone buying this round man a rainbow choice of braces. She looks in the passenger mirror. At first glance, she could pass for a student, she supposes. She has worry lines, sure, what mum doesn't? But her short haircut – more to get rid of the fuss than any vanity project – serves to make her look, well, gamine. She doesn't look forty-four, but does it matter anyway? People don't look at you the same, once life has dug its sharp edges into you. Does it matter that you used to have adventures, that you wanted to go out and see the world? Fell in love with someone you were going to do it all with? No, individual stories might not matter at all, with time.

Hits from the 80s and 90s play on the radio while they wait. She had forgotten the easy banter of the British DJs. Don't they ever stop talking? She doesn't recognise the names they drop, although it's clear they are a bit celebrity obsessed. And the adverts! Did they always have so many ads interrupting the music? It is different in Madeira, where everything is a lot slower and less, well, urban. She has a feeling that the UK wouldn't suit her anymore.

The lorry moves up a space then stops. Bill tries to make conversation. 'You're a photographer, then?'

'I used to be. Now I work in a library. A photo library. We document the collection.'

'Collection? Sounds posh.'

'Not really. It's a small place. Pretty humble.'

'In Portugal, you said?'

'Um-hmm.'

'But you're heading to Paris?'

'Yes, for my son.'

'In the hospital, you said. You must be worried.'

She doesn't reply. It's obvious anyway.

He reaches over to open the glove compartment. Tissues, CDs and empty packages of Smarties fall out. He looks embarrassed but still rummages in the depths of the compartment to find what he is looking for: a 5 x 7 photo enclosed in a light acrylic frame.

He looks at it with a tender expression, then passes it to Lena. The colour is faded with a yellow tinge due to heat or time or both, but it is still readable. The group is posed in a studio with a simple grey background. There is a slightly slimmer version of Bill at a younger age, with a round woman and six children. The woman has ginger hair, is smiling widely, and wears a red Christmas jumper. The children range in ages from about one to perhaps thirteen. Some have the ginger hair of the mum, others have darker hair and more olive complexions. All of them are wearing some variation of the Christmas jumper; a younger girl has a snowman bow in her hair.

'Six children?'

'My wife likes kids,' he says.

'How old are they now?'

'Oh, this was taken such a long time ago, when Leo was just a year old. He's ten now. But they're not all our natural children.' He takes the photo and puts it back in the compartment, shoving in the sweets and tissues. 'We fostered, too. The second and third eldest were fostered. We had them for years, when we thought we couldn't have any more children. After Joe was born, you see, there were complications.'

Lena wonders if she can prevent all the medical discussion that men sometimes assume mothers are interested in. Thankfully, he glosses over it.

155

'Fostering, though,' he says, 'it can break your heart. But super rewarding. Have you ever considered it?'

She shakes her head.

'You fall in love with these kids. Hell, I believe you can love any child that God gives you responsibility for. That's what I think. Genetics is only one of the things that bind you together as a family. I really believe that. And when we had Jenny and August given to our care, we just loved them like the other children. Sure, they had problems. August had night terrors for years. I put in earplugs when I was sleeping at home because otherwise I wouldn't be safe driving. But my wife had no unbroken night of sleep for, like, twelve years.'

From his profile she watches his bottom lip tighten to stifle emotions. He takes a few breaths before continuing. 'August was torn between his birth family and us. We would have adopted him, really we would have. But they kept saying that he should go back. For the child benefit, that's all they wanted. They didn't care about the boy, about his schooling or friendships or terrors. It was such a shame. It can make you all very cynical, when that's how decisions are made about a child's life and wellbeing.

'We had no choice, really. When he was fifteen, they made us give him back, but we always told him he had an open door to us. And he used it, a few times. We lived near enough, in Folkestone it's all pretty close anyway. We knew the family and kept hoping that they'd turn themselves around. But it all ended...' His voice trails off and they reach the barrier at the front of the lorry queue.

They hand their passports to the customs officer. Lena hopes that her last-minute details written on the customs declaration form won't raise any kind of alarm. The officer motions for Bill to move the truck to the side bay. He gets out to open up the back and show that he is carrying what was declared.

She looks out of the window at the hundreds of cars and lorries and motorcycles all hoping to get aboard the next boat. The back of the ferry is open and it's like looking into the bowels of a whale. A mechanical one, with rusting angles and parking spaces allocated for lorries and cars with impatient drivers. To the side she can see the pedestrian traffic: people wheeling bicycles, out for an adventure. There is a large group of teenagers with backpacks on some kind of journey.

That's what Bene should be doing right now, she thinks. Spending time travelling with his friends, seeing Europe by sea or rail. Not in a hospital room in a foreign country. She had pushed him to take this journey. He was doing it for her, because she never had the courage to do it by herself.

So many regrets, and she's not used to feeling that way about Bene. They have always been a team, playing for the same side. More and more often, she let him counsel her on what to do, and he would be right. And now she's leaned on him to do the one thing she could not, and this is what has happened.

There are some family vehicles packed to the brim with people and things, the pillows and stuffed toys pressed against the window. Was it the start of holidays? No, too early. Unless things have changed, UK schools don't break up until mid-July, right? She wonders if it feels the same as when she was growing up. The days in June that dragged on, when the summer weather – if it wasn't raining – made it too hot to sit still. As a child she would daydream and forget what the teacher was saying. She was told off all the time. Didn't stop her dreaming and wishing for summer to come and stay.

As a teenager she'd lost the habit of wishing for summer. She had fallen in love with something else: the darkroom. Her parents were amazed that she would voluntarily go down into the depths of the art college and work at the photo lab for hours at a time. Choosing the chemical-soaked environment of photographic processes over the fleeting summer sunshine.

She remembers the feeling of coming out of the lab one long summer day just after sunset. She sensed the moisture in the air as the temperature settled down from the height of the heat. She heard the traffic and sirens and other sounds that spoke of a London summer. She had missed her chance in the sun, and it left her feeling giddy, pale and strangely satisfied. She blinked away the surprise that day had turned into evening without her knowledge. Her stomach was empty and her head was dizzy; she'd forgotten to eat lunch. That's what happens when you focus all your attention on the minute details that affect an image. Also, no food was allowed in the darkroom. One crumb or speck of dust could ruin a picture if you didn't catch it.

She missed a whole summer that way. Her friends didn't understand. She was alone in her pursuit, until university. Even then, she was pretty much alone. She never quite found a way to define her art in a way that stood up to the others spouting the history of surrealism, or political theories about power, or whatever. She never got into that. Maybe because she didn't see it as art. She didn't describe herself as an artist either. She saw herself more as a witness. A still-documentary maker, if there was such a thing. So she didn't fit in, not in art college.

No, she was a photographer who got her lucky break in Africa. She became a kind of photojournalist, for a time. And then it all fell apart. Because she couldn't handle the intensity. She burned out, couldn't hack it. There was nothing spectacular, no fireworks. It ended in a cry rather than a bang. It had to change, because of Bene. The small fact of his existence. But she didn't resent him for it. In fact, she was grateful. Thanks to him, she had a reason to live.

She's been doing everything not to think of him. She bites her lip and swallows down a sob. You'll reach France, she tells herself. Bill says he'll drop her in Lille and then she'll get to Paris somehow. You'll make it to his bedside and his eyes will open, his beautiful brown eyes, so dark that that you could never see the pupils. And he'll say his characteristic 'Hiya!' And you'll see that he'll be alright.

She shouldn't have let him travel alone. Seventeen is still quite young. Although anyone who knows the boy sees that he is wise beyond his years. Always has been. Even when he was a young kid, he was attempting to read Aunt Magda's sailing magazines because there were not many kids' magazines. You had to take the boy seriously, just from his earnestness. As a single mum, she relied on that.

She doesn't remember his childhood as a stretch of time but rather as punctuated moments; documented in photographs pinned to the wall or hastily pasted into photo albums. For two separate people, they were often in a strange kind of sync. They couldn't explain it to themselves or anyone else. But people saw it, murmured under their breath. It was a blessing, really, to have a son who understood his mum on a deep level. Questions didn't have to be asked; personalities were symbiotic. She gave him a safe space to grow, and he would come running in with the new surprises or learnings to share.

Maybe Bill is right, and you would love anyone that God gave you responsibility for. She can't judge – she just has Bene. God gave her the one child, and all the responsibility.

'Hang on, Bene,' she says. She feels the back door of the lorry slam and sees Bill walk back to the cab. He is nodding his head, confident.

'I'm coming as soon as I can,' she whispers. 'Wait for me!'


There is a storm brewing in France, which is causing delays to the ferries. But her boat is now in motion. On the upper deck of the boat, she looks out towards the continent. The air is thick with moisture and the rain will come soon.

She can't see any signs of land ahead, and it's dark. The sun won't set until around ten. There are clear skies over England. But she has no desire to look back. She needs to focus her energy forwards, on getting to Bene.

She's forgotten this feeling that England has, when the summer sun is behind evening clouds. It's not the same in Madeira. She supposes it's because of the latitude, England being that much closer to the Arctic Circle. She's not used to the big seasonal shifts anymore, where the sun sets after ten in the summer, and before four in the winter.

The boat engines are loud and steady. She feels vibrations through the thin soles of her shoes. She rests her elbows on the railings and feels it there too. She looks down at the heavy edge of the metal cutting through the water. The wake behind is frothy and jagged. The water is unsettled with the coming storm.

The mist changes in character. Drops cling to her eyelashes and make her vision blurry at the periphery. She still can't see France. She can't even see ahead of the boat. Just the knife's line of the metal slicing the waves, the darkness shunted away.

She remembers another boat, another time. She had morning sickness compounding the seasickness, all she could do was hold onto the railings and keep looking at the horizon. People told her to close her eyes, but that only made her feel worse. She kept seeing images of the past when she did that, of the men on horseback, burning tents, Hiba shouting about the attack on her sister, and being trapped in a car sliding through mud. Better to keep her eyes open, feeling the breeze come and make her try to blink. She needed the oxygen. It soothed every sense – nose, throat, skin, the eyes too.

She had never felt like that before or since – like a thing growing inside of her was threatening to turn her inside out. It was potentially a good thing, a beautiful thing, but it didn't necessarily feel benign.

In the days ahead of going to Madeira, she had felt outside herself. It was like she was somebody else, looking down at a woman on a bewildering path of choices, running away from what she had known. She didn't care about herself, her relationships or her career. But she found a sense of purpose: to protect the child.

She had an instinct she hadn't known she possessed. She alone would have to protect the baby, whatever it turned out to be; boy or girl, she wasn't bothered. But it was fragile, and needed to be taken out of danger. Not like what happened before, with the miscarriage. It wasn't her fault, she didn't know a baby was on the way. But this time she knew, so she had to do what was right.

Heaving on the boat to Madeira, refusing all offers of food or medicine. She was on her knees with her head in a bucket and some kind strangers holding back her hair.

Why did she let strangers help? Where was Kojo? Why didn't she bring him into the story, give him some responsibility?

She doesn't have an answer. It went so deep, this instinct to protect her unborn child. Deeper roots than romance, than sexual attraction. More important than their work or plans or travel. It gave her a sense of the future. But that future depended on her turning her back on her current situation. She had to escape, following the one impulse: to flee.

# Part IV

# Twenty-two

## Bene

### Paris, 22 June 2022

That beeping noise. It's faint, but always there. What is it? It sounds like one of those birds that get confused as to whether it is day or night. Maybe with a late spring or something. The birds that cheep after dusk or at 3 am. Desperate to find a mate. Get a sense of time, man!

Why can't he turn over to cover his ears with the pillow? Inside his eyelids he feels a heaviness that means he needs sleep. But he is a bit alarmed too. Why can't he move? Is he dreaming?

His head is fuzzy. His thoughts jump around and are jumbled. Was it too much to drink? And that damn bird, still chirping. Or maybe it's not a bird. Maybe one of those lorries is taking too long to back up around a corner or something. Jesus, it's annoying.

What day is it? He's sleeping, so it must be night, but which night? He tries to remember what happened.

Fatima. He remembers her smile, her dark curls. Her lips, full and wet. She licked them when she talked, like she knew he wanted to kiss her. She kept talking, and he tried to listen. He really did try. But all he could think about were those lips, and how he was going to find a break in her flow of words and kiss her.

Did he make a fool of himself in front of her? He can't remember. That means he had too much to drink, or maybe the drink was stronger than he realised. He can't remember if there were that many. Shit, something went wrong. Were the drinks spiked? He'd read something about that. A foreigner in a strange city, the girl spikes his drink then robs him blind.

But Fatima wasn't like that. Nothing about her was like that. She was older, sophisticated, connected in this city. Classy, way out of his league. And anyway, he has nothing to steal. Just a passport and his digital camera. Mum would be really cross if he lost that. Actually, he'd be more pissed off than she would. He'd have to save up for a new one, and now that the summer has started, the chance of getting a well-paying job is close to nil.

Where is Fatima now? Did they do more than kiss? Why can't he remember anything?

The beeping continues. He wonders if it's one of those car alarms in the distance. He read about that once, how some scientist took his research to the companies that make car alarms. He was hired because he'd worked in the rainforest for so long, he could recognise all sorts of cries of tropical birds. And he then picked the most annoying one and turned it into a car alarm that it's not humanly possible to ignore. Nature. Out to destroy your sanity if you let it.

Suddenly his head feels heavier, like it's tipping back. His body feels like it is sinking down at a different pace than his head. He can't figure out where he is in space but he's thinking too slowly to panic.

He feels a vibration in his throat and hears a low moan. Then there's a rustling noise, somebody putting down a magazine or papers or something. He wants to say something to the person. About the car alarm. About how heavy his head is. But he can't say anything. He can't seem to open his lips. Another moan pushes its way out of his throat but he doesn't control it.

He hears footsteps, walking away, and a door opening. More footsteps, and a few different voices. He can make out only snatches of words.

'*Le niveau de morphine est bas... Pas confortable... On manque l'accord parental...*'

He doesn't understand these people or what they're doing here. It sounds like French. Is he in Paris? Or did he make it to Kenya? Is his dad coming? He wants to cry, like in a dream where everything is going wrong but you don't know when the dream will end. It will end though, won't it?

He wishes Mum was there to wake him up, in the way she did when he was young and had nightmares about the storms. Always the same dream, about the storm hitting the house. Lashes of rain harder than nails hammering the windows, threatening to break through. But she always seemed to know when it was happening, and how to wake him just before it became too real.

# Kojo

### Paris

He has no plan, no guide. He is at the Gare du Nord with no sense of where to go next. He tries to piece the information together with his patchwork of French, but feels as helpless as a child.

Why did he never learn the language properly? Like Kumi. The perfect son. The shining older brother. So many things would have been better for Kojo if he had followed his brother's example.

He doesn't know why the memory of Kumi jumps into his mind whenever he feels uncertain. Like now, trying to read the signs in French. When he is nervous or hesitant, there comes Kumi's image right in front of him. It's so stupid. As if Kumi has never been nervous or unsure. He is just a man; you would think by now Kojo would know that and move on. But for some reason, the impressions from childhood remain indelible.

He has an address for the hospital, but one look at the Metro map leaves him paralysed with apprehension. What if he goes in the wrong direction and ends up miles away? No, he needs to exchange some money and get a taxi.

He walks through the rail station to the money exchange and feels eyes on him. Looking around, though, he can't see from where. Paris is such a strange city. There are a lot of Africans here, but there is a palpable mistrust. It's not a welcoming place. It's as if the French have had some collective bad experience and can't see past that. Especially if you don't make an effort to learn the language.

Or maybe he's just being paranoid. What would Kumi do? He would hold his head high. Kojo remembers the lectures he used to have to endure from his father and brother. 'You're Ashanti!' they would say, talking louder than necessary to make the point. 'Have some pride!'

There was always the implicit criticism. That to have any doubt about yourself meant letting the family down. You had to always be sure of yourself, hold yourself with confidence. Or else you were letting the family pride slip. Instead of building it up, you were allowing life to erode it at the foundations, making the mausoleum start to crumble. It was your fault, you see, if you weren't like them. If you didn't keep the family tradition going. It was your fault if you didn't build on that legacy. No matter what you did, if you didn't contribute to that, then you were nothing. Not nothing exactly, but a disappointment. Better to be an absence than a disappointment.

The rain outside is torrential and he is unprepared. Europe in summer, it should be warm, shouldn't it? But no. A cold rain makes a mockery of his assumptions. He doesn't have a coat. Only packed one blazer, and it is already soaked. No umbrella. No hat to keep the rain off him. He should have grabbed a newspaper at least. He feels the drops slide down, curving around his brow and falling onto his cheeks and lips. He blows out his frustration with puffs.

There are no taxis at the taxi queue, only a long line of people. Kojo presses his breast pocket where the address to the hospital is hopefully still safe. He doesn't know what he is doing here in Paris, or how he will approach this boy. A teenager, really. Is he the arrogant type, pretending to be a man? Or a humble one, looking up to his elders? If he's anything like Lena, he'll be a paradox. Someone totally foreign to him.

But if this boy is his, as Jeanette says, then some parts of him must be recognisable. He wonders what elements of his family line he has transmitted to this boy. What characteristics took root? Others, probably, wilted and didn't thrive in the European climate. But there would be some things, surely, to link father to son. He wonders if it will be obvious, or difficult to sense.

He has no idea what he's going to say to this boy. Or to Lena. In fact, he doubts the wisdom of being here at all. He should have called. Or written a letter. Demanded an explanation. Because although his main emotion is curiosity and concern, he feels the acid of unanswered anger burn in the back of his throat. It is feeding on a sense of injustice, and it won't go away.

# Twenty-three

**Bene**

There's that noise again. But sleep is still holding onto him, a bit too long. Bene can't open his eyes but doesn't feel any urgency. Maybe he will in a moment.

He thinks of the girl with the nose-ring and a long chain connecting it to her earring. He remembers not liking her then for that. Not sure why. He doesn't mind other jewellery. Has even wondered about getting an ear piercing himself. Gil tried to do it one evening as a joke. Lucky for him he slid over just in time for Gil to lunge forward and pierce the back of the leather sofa instead. They'd laughed so hard at that one.

The girl kept going in circles, dancing with herself. In the shadow of the Eiffel Tower, he remembers now. She must have been on E. Did she slip one to him, when he wasn't looking? No... it would've taken effect beforehand, surely. He remembers watching her, in a happy world all of her own, and wondering what it felt like in her veins. Did she really have an unending wave of happiness, just from a pill? He couldn't believe it was possible. Or actually, he did believe it was possible, but there would always be a price.

Some hidden or not-so-hidden cost for that heightened level of happiness. Maybe you had to sell off your first-born son or something.

He remembers being at the base of the Eiffel Tower, and the sketchbook in his lap. Charcoal, it was. Or pencil? He can't seem to focus on what was in his left hand. Why can't he remember?

He can see the people pitching souvenirs. They were laying out their blankets of trinkets for tourists. Also somewhere else... yes, outside the Pyramid. Loads of them – maybe eight or nine, all of them African. Their skin was a dark blue-black, not a mixed brother amongst them. They joked together, knowing they were all in the same boat.

He remembers those African men as if they were standing in front of him right now. They wore plain clothes in maroons and browns, and jeans, like anyone else. He knows they were assessing him, trying to place him. Does he fit in their category? No, skin too pale, twists too short. He was a kid playing tourist with a little bit of money to spend. Not like them. Who knows what their stories were? Crossing the Mediterranean or the Atlantic or the Sahara, who knows? Hell, what does he know? They could have been born right here in Paris, just found that selling to tourists is a better way to earn a living than something else. He can't pretend to know what goes on in these men's lives. They might have a story similar to his father's, for all that he knows.

His father. All Bene has are those photos of him. He looks like a nice guy, a bit tired in the eyes maybe. He shared the photos with Fatima last night. Was it last night? They joked about baldness being hereditary. Will his hair go that way as well? Doesn't show any sign of it at the moment, but you never know. He hopes he has a good long time before any of that happens.

Fatima had thought that he had the same profile as the man. She had said it before kissing him on the tip of his nose.

He told her everything. Too much. He talks too much when he's excited, he knows that about himself. After he had showed her the photos, he tried to explain why he wasn't mad.

Fatima didn't understand. 'I'd be furious,' she said.

'You don't get it, that's just my mum's way.'

'I never would have allowed it,' she said with authority. 'I never would have let so many years pass without telling me the truth.'

'She didn't lie,' he tried to explain. He felt protective. 'She just didn't feel like the time was right to tell me the whole story. Not when I was young.'

'That's the same thing as lying, telling just part of the truth.'

'Not the same. Degrees of difference.'

She looked at him, eyes suddenly narrowing like a girl feeling she'd made a mistake. 'I've said too much. She's your mum. You want to defend her.'

'No, no.' He shifts to put the photographs back into his backpack. 'Let's talk about you instead.'

'Me? There's nothing special about me. I don't get to go anywhere.'

'What do you mean? Everything is special about you.' He didn't even know what he was saying. He would say anything, just to be kissing her again.

# Kojo

The colours of Paris fly past his window, now that he has managed to catch a taxi. He apologises to the driver, noticing the drops of rain from his clothes landing on the cab's leather seats. He doesn't try to make conversation, just shows the man the paper with the name of the hospital.

He shivers in the back seat. The air conditioning is on, even though it's not a hot day. Maybe it keeps the windscreen from fogging up, but it's not working very well. He rubs his sleeve on the window to see out.

Paris is a beautiful city, he has to admit. It is orderly and majestic, at least in this section. He likes the sense of history in the buildings, the national pride.

At the same time, he misses Nairobi. The disorder that laces the side of the highways when you drive. The crowds that try to swallow you when you walk into the marketplace. You're always on your guard against pickpockets or worse, but you also know that you can move around as you like. He can slide through the tightly packed tangle of humanity, he knows the way. It's become his home, and he wishes he were there right now.

He can't say why – is it the house? Coming home to Paradisa's cooking and Omondi's stories about school? He struggles to remember what they spoke about yesterday; it was a day like any other with the boy folded close over his homework. He'll have to see if Omondi's glasses prescription is strong enough. Maybe it needs changing. He'll mention it to Paradisa as soon as he gets back.

He didn't have a chance to say goodbye to the boy. He left a note to both of them. Promising to be back very soon. Paradisa would be surprised to get it, although she wouldn't say anything. He can see her now, folding the paper and putting it into the front pocket of her apron. She wouldn't like it, that there would now be too much food prepared. It could go off, and she hates letting anything go to waste. Maybe she will take the leftovers to her church for Bible study night. Lord knows, the people there will appreciate it.

He'll be back soon. He knows his home is there. This will be a short visit; just something he has to do. Tying up loose ends from long ago. Squaring the circle, that's what Lena used to say. It made him laugh, the way she said that. Very matter-of-fact, as if squaring circles was what everybody wanted to do. He challenged her about it once, demanding that she explain what it meant. She claimed that was impossible, it was just a British saying from her youth. They descended into laughter at the absurdity of it, and ever since then he'd thought of her when people said that, about circles. Or about any task that seemed absurd to one person, and straightforward to somebody else.

She has that way of creeping into his thoughts. Less often now that so many years have passed. But still, some eighteen years on, he often glimpses a reminder of something they used to talk about. Or some aspect that was particular to her and no one else in the world. Like the way she made a tight ring with her fist when looking out at a landscape, looking through it like an old-fashioned camera. He'd laugh at that, called it her telescoping. She would laugh too. They could do that, laugh at themselves and each other, without malice.

Something in her got damaged, he sees that now. She lost some of that laughter, the ability to just let it flow over and out of her. After those last trips to Darfur, she lost something. She was jumpy, and snapped at small things. Things he said, and other people. Snapped when things went wrong, as they sometimes did. The electricity faltering. The car failing to start in a dark parking lot after dinner out. It was as if she had a heightened sense of threat, and couldn't adjust back to the daily rhythm of life in a busy city.

It was physical too. One time a matatu backfired a few cars ahead, and she jumped as if someone had shot a gun. For that split second he saw a woman truly terrified. Pinned to her seat, reaching for her seatbelt as if she was unsure whether to depend on it or to release it and run.

He saw all this from his peripheral vision, and it scared him. She had this animal instinct in her, to run, and he could see it but could not relate to it. He had no such instinct. It was as if they were wired differently, and at some point her innate wiring might cross and then she would detonate like a bomb.

And that's perhaps what she feared, too. They never talked about it, those moments when she was petrified from a fear that seemed out of all proportion to the cause. It was something in her that he could not soothe, and could not reach. He assumed that she would keep it under wraps, or ask for help if it was getting out of control. But instead, she decided to let it rule and ran off with it. Like a lover, taking her away from him. Leaving him with nothing but questions, despair and regret.

# Twenty-four

## Bene

**Paris, the night before**

The clanging of the garage door interrupted their embrace. They moved slightly apart and opened their eyes. Fatima smiled at him, but then looked away, listening to the new arrivals.

'*Merde*,' she said, and let go of Bene.

'What is it?'

'Raphael, Aisha's ex. He's trouble.'

'What do you mean, trouble?'

'You know, bad news. Raphael has always been a nightmare.' She moved away from him slightly.

'A nightmare, I always wondered about that. How can a person be a nightmare? They're just one person. A nightmare is something like a scene in a movie, somewhere you're trapped in and can't get out. Or an atmosphere, like a storm coming and you have no shelter.'

'Like now?' She gestured up at the clouds. 'They said it was going to rain tonight.'

'Who said? I don't think so.'

'Are you crazy? Smell the air! You know what's coming.'

'I have no idea what's coming.' He leaned closer to her. 'But I'm hoping it's something nice.'

She leaned into him, but her focus was down. He looked at the top of her eyelids, fringed by the black lashes, and wondered if she was thinking the same things he was. How he wanted to just freeze time and stay exactly where they were, and kiss her until the sun came up.

'He was really bad news,' she said.

'Who?' he sat back a little. She obviously wasn't thinking about the same thing.

'Raphael. Shit, there he is.'

A group of men came through the courtyard. One of them led the way. The guy wore a brimmed hat, tipped slightly forward, and carried a leather bag diagonally across his body. He spoke quickly and quietly to the group behind him. He stopped to rub out a cigarette with his shoe and paused before the plate glass door.

'*Salut*, Tima,' he called to her.

'*Salut*,' she replied quietly, looking down at her hands.

The men walked into the party, leaving the door ajar. For a few moments there was no movement. Bene watched Fatima closely as she breathed a jagged breath in, and then gave the sigh of an exhale. He wanted to see if she would speak first, so he continued to watch. Shaky breath in, sigh out.

'What are you staring at?' she said, standing up abruptly.

# Kojo

The hospital is a huge red brick building with a chimney stack like a watchtower looming above the entrance. It looks like a prison. Why would they build a hospital like that? Maybe it was a prison first, then changed use later when they needed hospital spaces. There's something militaristic about it that repels him. He hesitates before opening the taxi door, but it's clear the driver is keen to move on to the next fare.

He pays and gets out. At least there is an awning here to keep him out of the rain. He feels awkward with his wheelie suitcase and drenched clothes. He should have left the case in a storage locker at the train station. Then he would have been lighter here, freer to move around easily. No chance of that now.

The luggage wheels squeak as he walks through the automatic glass doors. Another wash of air conditioning comes over him as he crosses the threshold. He's going to catch something if they keep this up.

He sees the round reception counter and a list of departments and treatment centres, arrows pointing in different directions. Colour coding for different wards. He has no idea what ward an adolescent boy would go to. Probably good to follow the red *URGENCE* signs at first. A head wound, that's what Jeanette had said. Not critical, but very serious. Poor child.

But he can't go and talk to the doctors like this, wet as a fish. He ducks into the men's room to change his clothes. Maybe it's just as well that he's kept his luggage with him. He doesn't have spare shoes, but he does have a change of shirt and trousers. Paradisa pressed the shirt at the weekend, and he'd slipped it hurriedly into the suitcase. Not perfectly folded – if she had helped him pack he knows it would have been immaculate. But it is passable. A tie? No, not necessary to be formal. This isn't a job interview; it is about meeting a teenager, making sure he is alright after his ordeal. He pulls on his only jumper and straightens his collar.

He should have brought something from Kenya, a souvenir from East Africa. Or if he'd known this was happening, he would have arranged for some fresh Kente cloth to be shipped. There are traditions you observe in his culture, ones he hasn't thought of in years. They are rituals for when a baby is born, and the lessons from father to son when he reaches the right age. These are the times when a father steps in to show a child what it means to be part of a family, to carry on a legacy. Also the other moments – the first day of school, the exams to get into a good college. These are the traditional and more modern moments, all of them missed with this boy named Bene. So many missed opportunities.

He looks at himself in the mirror. His skin seems grey. His eyes are bloodshot, from the air conditioning and the overnight flight. He rubs some cocoa butter on his face and neck, the muscles at the back of his head tense. He rubs his knuckles into the front of each shoulder and rolls his head.

How did he turn into a man who has a son he never knew? Would another man, a stronger one, a better man, have known? He should have known. He should have found out the truth from Lena, about why she left. He should have held on to her more tightly, insisted that he was strong enough to protect her and their child. There must be something missing in him. Something he lacks. Surely a father should know when his flesh and blood comes into the world, no?

Lena accused him once of something. What was it? A lack of empathy. She said it with nearly closed lips, so quiet he barely heard it. What was it about? He can't even remember now. Maybe there is something missing in him. Fifty-eight years old now, and there has been only one woman who's touched him deeply, who woke him up from apathy and made him care. She was the only one who had everything – the sexual energy, the potent questions, the laughter, the understanding of his work, the comprehension of him, body and mind.

And yet she slipped away without a word and kept this secret for eighteen years. He's been numb ever since. He sees that now.

How could she have done this to him? His emotions are in such turmoil he doesn't know if he wants to rip the sink off the wall, or cry into the basin like a man beaten.

# Twenty-five

## Bene

He watched Fatima as she went back into the party. Should he have walked away then? Gone back to the hostel, left behind the kiss and the memories of the night, keeping only the photos as souvenirs? Probably.

His camera, where was his camera? He looked around where they'd been sitting and it was not there. He must have left it inside when they were part of the drum circle. He couldn't leave without his camera, his backpack too. That would be a complete screw up.

He came through the patio door, and found her in the kitchen, hip to hip with Aisha. They were leaning into each other like two halves of a tree braided together after years of coexistence. Their black curls blended; it was a wonder they didn't get snarled. Their solidarity was clear. Fatima's smile was gone; Aisha's mouth was set in a flat line despite the heavy lipstick decorating its fullness. Worry lines laced the sides of Fatima's eyes, and her brow had that line between that meant anger.

Raphael and his friends stood on the other side of the kitchen. He'd turned down the brim of his hat to deliberately block the girls out of his view. Bene could see his smirk. The guys murmured in low tones. It was not clear why they were there. Were they forcing themselves into somewhere they weren't wanted? Had they been welcome in the past, but no longer? Were they making a point? Taking a stand? Bene had the feeling he was watching some kind of standoff about to take place. Was it provocation or trying to make up?

No one was looking at Bene. He could have been invisible. Suddenly it was the worst feeling in the world, like you didn't exist. You never existed for these people. They walked around you, looked through you, like that plate glass door. He looked back and saw that he had left it open. He reached to slide it back shut, as any polite guest would.

'*Ça va, frère?*' said someone near him. Bene looked up and saw a guy about his age, the same black bouncy curls as the girls', just shorter. He wore a black t-shirt and a smile.

'*Il ne comprend pas le français,*' Fatima said.

Bene tried to object with his schoolboy memory. 'No, I do understand. *Je comprends, un peu. Mais pas trop...*' He looked at the guy, hoping for some understanding.

'You're English?'

Bene shrugged. It was easier than explaining it all again.

The guy came forward with his hand outstretched. 'That's brilliant!' He spoke with the accent of someone schooled by the British. 'I'm going to study in Manchester in the autumn! I'm Samy, and this is Noah. Fatima's our sister.'

Bene took the hand, amused by the formality. This guy must have been studying an old textbook about manners or something. But there was something about the kid he instantly liked. Maybe it was the way that Fatima looked up once they started talking.

Samy asked about his trip, and Bene tried to remember if he was supposed to be playing a certain part here or if he could just relax. He decided to strike a balance, saying that he was coming from Portugal, heading out to

Nairobi to see his father. He didn't add that he'd never met the man before in his life.

'That's cool,' Samy said. 'Nairobi's supposed to be awesome. The music scene there is brilliant. But have you been to Marrakech?'

Bene shook his head. There was so much of the world he hadn't seen yet. He felt like a kid all of a sudden.

'The DJs coming out of that place are amazing, mixing it up with grime from London and blending in traditional rhythms like *chaabi* or *raï*. There's nothing like it.' He took out his phone and scrolled through some songs. 'Here, I'll play you some. It's in French, but you can get a sense of their rhythm. The rhythm, man!' He pounded on his chest a few times like it was a drum. 'It's all Afrobeats lately. Or Afro-grime.'

The music started from the phone, but Bene couldn't hear. He pointed to the drum circle next door.

'Of course, let's go outside.' Samy slid the garden door to the side again and gestured for Bene to step out. Noah made to come out as well, but paused to reach back and take three beers.

Bene remembered his camera and backpack in the drumming room, but figured there was no harm in taking a moment with the brothers. It might help him with Fatima, and anyway, it was always good to hear some new tunes.

They settled back on the chairs that Fatima and Bene had sat in earlier. Samy's back was to the kitchen, but Bene could see the profile of Fatima and Aisha from where he sat.

Samy found the band he was looking for. He rattled off statistics about when they formed, what the full album was like. He was hoping to catch them in a concert once he was studying in England.

Bene stopped listening to Samy, and let the music sink in. It was melodic, and had a definite Arab feel. The words, when they came, hit like blows. He couldn't understand; it was too fast and furious. It was like an urban boxing match. But there was only one voice, so maybe it was a boxer by himself. Calling out rhymes into the darkness, putting jabs into the bag and shouting to prove he wasn't alone.

# Kojo

After a few wrong turns, Kojo finds the ward for adolescents. He walks through the automatic doors, wheeling his bag like a muddy dog trailing behind him.

From the nurses' station, there are rows of doors for rooms extending out in different directions. He asks for the room for Benedito Rodrigues. Jeanette had reminded him to use Lena's last name. Of course, the child has his mother's name. No trace of the Ghanaian line at all.

The nurse points to the far corridor and makes a few gestures, speaking in very fast French. He doesn't understand much of what she says, but he knows that '*vingt-deux*' means twenty-two. He nods as if all is understood and walks briskly in the indicated direction. As soon as the corridor bends out of sight, he slows down and takes a breath.

Door 22 is no different from all the others. There is a small rectangular window in an otherwise opaque frame. He hears various noises and beeps and the sound of metal scraping on a hard floor. Is that from the boy's room, or another? The hushed sounds of the ventilation system flow in pipes above his head.

He stands away from the door, unable to commit. Who is this boy? Does he know anything about his father? What has Lena said, or not said, over the years? Will he be disappointed in Kojo if they meet?

There are chairs lined up on the opposite wall, a bit away from the door. Kojo moves back and sits down in a rush. His heart is beating wildly and his hand shakes as he clutches the suitcase. Letting go of the bag, he drops his arms into his lap. He squeezes his thighs for a moment to try to get a grip.

He looks down at his hands. The tops of them are wrinkled like those of any other fifty-eight-year-old man. They are the same dark brown they always have been. Turning them over, the paler skin appears underneath. He still has the rows of callouses. Like barnacles, they attached themselves to him over his years of labour as an engineer and never rubbed off. Lena thought they would, but then what did she know about a man growing old? Nothing, at least not from him. She hasn't shared any of the journey with him. Just left him behind.

His breathing slows down and he tries to get some sense back. What is he afraid of? A young man, a boy really. Got himself in trouble and now the French health care system will sort him out. He'll be fine. He's obviously a bit foolhardy, probably not making the right choices. His mother will be worried, disappointed. Probably never was strict enough with him. Probably didn't know anything about raising a boy, when it all started.

He stands up again, leaving the suitcase there. He'll just take a look through the window. No one is around, he won't intrude.

Peering inside, he can't see very well. A curtain is pulled around the hospital bed, shrouding the patient's face and head. How does he know it's even Bene? Maybe he heard the wrong room number. Inside are two women, and Jeanette said he was travelling alone. The women are young, girls really. Well, maybe one is older than the other. They both have long black curls that bounce when they turn. And there's a boy, standing with them. He's not ill, so it can't be Bene. He's Arab, like the girls. You can tell from the face shape, the slim body-type.

One of the girls stands with her back against the far wall. If she raises her eyes she will see him. But she doesn't look up. Her eyes remain on the floor, as if there's nothing to hope for. She has her arms crossed, cupping her elbow with one hand. With the other hand she rolls her thumb against her forefinger, not stopping. Maybe she's a smoker, longing for a cigarette.

He can't see the face of the other girl who is sitting near the edge of the bed. Her hair is like a shield, but he can read her body language – curved down, elbows in, one hand reaching forward. A worried posture. Someone with no control in a situation bigger than she is.

She reaches forward and holds a hand that lies still on top of the sheets. That's all he can see: this arm. A forearm of smooth light-brown-coloured skin. It doesn't look Ghanaian. He's nothing like him, this light-skinned boy. No faults to be seen. And no movement in the hand.

He must be out of it, Kojo decides. No point in being there when the boy isn't even conscious. The girls, well, they would know him even less than the boy does. He goes back and sits down by his suitcase. Through the window, he can still see the top of the sitting girl's head, but nothing else.

Suddenly, the girl jumps up. Kojo sees her lean forward, revealing the profile of a beautiful young woman. Kojo stands up too, unsure what to do. The girls are speaking to each other in very fast French. They sound alarmed, their voices getting louder.

The older girl opens the door in a rush, calling for a doctor. She looks left and right in the hallway, and seeing no one else, her eyes rest on Kojo for a fraction of a second. He sees that she shares the other woman's beauty, but her face is stained by makeup smudged from crying. They lock eyes for a second, and she quickly assesses that he is not a doctor. He looks away, pretending not to be involved.

She runs past Kojo to the nurses' station, shouting words he does not understand. The room door shuts behind her, leaving him no wiser.

I can't handle this, he thinks. I have no place here. Lena cut me out eighteen years ago, when she left me to have this child alone. I have no responsibility for him, and in turn he and his friends owe me nothing, not even an explanation. I am a stranger to him. I need to leave. Right away.

# Twenty-six

## Lena

The train pulls out of Lille, heading towards Paris. She is glad to be on the move again. She hasn't showered or eaten in a long time. She should take better care of herself. Maybe she'll get a bit of sleep here before they get into Gare du Nord. No chance of a shower, but she could at least wash her face.

In the WC she sees the 'no drinking' symbol over the basin and reconsiders. She doesn't want to put that water on her face. Better not. The toilet bowl has water that is an unnatural blue, full of chemicals. It's like the blue that Bene used to love, rejecting all other colours. He was funny like that. As a young boy, already very excited by drawing, he went through a very rigid phase. Totally unlike what he became later. But for a short time, when he was three maybe, he only wanted that shade of blue. Royal blue. Superman blue, he called it. Drew and coloured and held the crayons and markers tight in his left hand. Didn't want any other colour, for about a year. But when he started school, he changed his mind and broadened out. Then he went in the other direction – wasn't happy unless he had all the colours of the rainbow, and more: gold, black, maroon, all sorts. He would take his paper and markers and spread out on the floor, making sure every colour, no matter what small fraction of a difference in shade, was represented in his wide rainbow.

There isn't any soap. She flicks her hands under the water, and then runs them through her hair to dry. She doesn't care what she looks like. No one is looking at her anyway. She walks back to her seat, thrown about by the movement of the train. When did that blue phase end? That is the problem with memories. You have these flashes of them like in a photograph, but then you go blurry on the details. She doesn't know if she's actually remembering a number of moments from his childhood together, or just the stories she's told him and herself over the years. About him and the Superman blue. And she's never had anyone else to hold her to the truth. What is the actual truth? Would Aunt Magda know?

No, Lena is alone. She chose to be alone, but years later that decision doesn't feel much like a choice. It feels like a line she's been forced to walk, a decision by whoever she was at the age of twenty-six. The person she used to be. Does she still want to be that person?

Bene's mum – absolutely. But Lena alone? No, not at all. But she doesn't know how to be any other way.

Bene, you'll be okay, she exhales in a small prayer. Do the other passengers notice? She doesn't care. He has to be okay. He's all she has. Without him, she is nothing. He is the best of her efforts, and the promise of a future. She can't imagine anything else. If anything happens to him... She wrenches her thoughts away. No mother can endure thinking that way for too long. It's not natural, goes totally against the rhythms of nature, a mother thinking about her son's mortality.

No, he'll be fine. The French hospitals are good, some of the best. And she'll be by his side soon. Lena and Bene, just like they always have been. Nothing can change that.

# Kojo

He sits on the closed toilet lid fully clothed. He needs space to think. No one to look at him. No one to judge him. Just breathe for a moment.

I can't do this, he thinks. I can't. I'm going to be sick. He feels dizzy. He wonders if he should move in case he vomits. But for some reason he can't shift himself. The position that feels most natural is this one: elbows on knees, head in his hands. He is a statue set in stone. There is a strong smell from the chemicals they use to clean. He hears the squeeze of some automatic spray above his head on a timer.

It's too intense. He can't meet this boy and then have him die. What a nightmare. He wishes he'd never heard of him. Never thought again of Lena. Never met Lena to begin with. Wishes she was never in his life.

No, he doesn't mean that. You can't erase people from your history. They make you who you are, at that moment and beyond. Who you become is built upon those moments, who you are in each small unit of time. The choices you make then, the people you choose to be with. The ones you love, and those who love you, including those who leave. And then you have to fix the damage yourself, build your own future.

That's what he's done all his life. Built himself back up, without the family to support his efforts. His own father was just a shadow to him after he left home. Kumi – criticising him, taking up all the praise, pushing him to the margins. Why was there never room for the two brothers, different, but each with some intrinsic value?

Lord knows he hasn't done badly. In any other family, humanitarian work and rising up to be the head of Africa region would be something to be proud of. Saving people's lives is worth something, surely.

The light in the toilets flickers off. For a moment, it is pure blackness. He is lost in space. He feels the shape of the toilet underneath him, puts his arms forward to feel the cubicle door. It's still there; it must just be that the light is motion-detected. He waves his arms, but nothing changes. He stands up, reaches for where the latch should be, and opens the door. The lights come back to life as if nothing has happened. He sees his lonely suitcase, resting by the sinks.

He looks in the mirror and sees the worried face of an old man. How has he come to this? He needs to get away from here. Can he leave without anyone knowing? He'll get another taxi back, all the way to the airport. He'll catch the next flight to Nairobi. Won't tell anyone. Only Jeanette will know, and he'll make her swear to secrecy. He won't have to tell Lena he was there, that he failed to find the courage to go in.

Paradisa would know – he had put it in the short letter. Why did he write all that? He should have just said it was a business trip, something that came up suddenly. She would have raised her eyebrows, but would've left it at that. They had an understanding. Nothing threatened that. As long as her Omondi was okay, growing and learning and bringing his stories and schooling back to their dining table at night, that would be enough.

He hadn't realised that until now. That is enough. Being in one boy's life. Being someone to that boy. He isn't a nobody. Through luck or chance, God brought Paradisa and Omondi into his life, and that is enough. They've made him the man he is today. They are waiting for him, back at home. He needs to get there, as soon as possible.

Relief floods through him and he feels light-headed. That's what he needs to do. He splashes water on his face and feels like he can face the world outside. He puts on his blazer, still damp with the rain, and gets ready to go home.

He opens the door, and senses something has changed. The door to room number 22 is ajar, and several doctors and nurses are standing around the bed, talking in raised voices. There is a lot of motion in the room, with beeping noises and equipment being wheeled around. It looks like a dance, this medical choreography to keep people alive.

Despite his conviction declared to the mirror, Kojo freezes. He can't leave without knowing. He moves closer to the door and tries to understand what's going on.

There are so many people in the room he can't see the patient. Instead, he sees the older girl, leaning again on the far wall. She is chewing on a fingernail, looking nervous but something in her eyes is happy. Cautious-happy. Kojo tries to see the other girl and the Arab boy but they are blocked by the doctors and nurses moving around. He hears different voices, all speaking French, and then a laugh from someone. Medium-pitched, it is the voice of an adolescent, not yet a man.

The curtain is pulled back and between the movements of the doctors Kojo sees that the boy is sitting up and awake. He has bandages over his forehead and one eye, wrapped all around the head like a mummy. The other eye has a purple ring below it and there are stripes of surgical tape on his cheek. But he is smiling. A wide, grateful smile, like someone who has been given an unexpected gift.

The boy speaks to the doctors and answers some questions. They reach out and take his pulse, check the beeping machines, testing and prodding him even though the evidence is clear: the boy is alright. He will be okay. Whatever happened last night, whatever happened with that girl in the streets of Paris that led him here and to his missing the plane to Nairobi, he is going to be okay.

That face, even with the bruises and stiches, Kojo has to admit that he is a handsome boy. Something in him looks like Lena, and also like Kumi. And something unique – totally his own. As if he has the confidence and luck to be anything in the world, and he just has to make the right choices.

Kojo can see why Jeanette said those things about him, why Lena would count so much on the boy's presence making any situation better. There is something about him that would make you hopeful, make you want to believe that the future will happen, and that, for this kid at least, the possibilities are beautiful.

Kojo comes out of the doorway. He doesn't belong here. He's satisfied that the doctors will do their job. It's time to go.

That's when he sees her. She comes down the corridor from the nurse's station, just like he did. She has a backpack, no roller suitcase. She somehow looks the same, yet totally different. Her black hair is cut short and has streaks of grey. She looks like she's slept in her clothes, but then Lena was never someone who cared what people thought about how she dressed. She is wearing plain sandals, no fussy shoes for her.

Her face is older and thinner. She has lines stretching across her forehead and ones around her mouth, making her cheekbones more prominent. The worry crease between her eyebrows is deep.

She doesn't see him at first. She is walk-running, reading the door numbers as she goes along. She is anxious, and her mouth looks like it has forgotten how to smile.

He steps away from the door to let her pass, and that's when she looks up at him. Her eyes are the same dark chocolate as years ago. A look on her face that's impossible to read in a moment – worry about her child, confusion about why he is there, worry about what he might think? Probably the worry for Bene eclipses all other thoughts.

She doesn't say a word, and looks past him into the room. The girls say something, and the doctor looks up. She sees her son, sitting up and smiling.

Kojo doesn't expect it, but she looks back at him then. And the look says it all. That there is far too much to explain, but he should know anyway. That she loved him once, but she had to do this alone.

She nods, and he does too.

He smiles widely and before he can help it, he is laughing. It starts small, but grows into a deep belly laugh. He laughs harder than he has in weeks.

He holds onto the doorframe and feels his eyes start to water as he gulps for breath and can't stop. Goodness knows what these people will think, this African man clinging to the wall and laughing until he's crying.

She laughs too. A quick, light laugh as she moves past him and pushes to her son's side. The boy says something Kojo can't hear and she embraces him, holding his bandaged head in her arms as she stands next to him. They make a strange couple, this smiling bandaged boy and the solo pixie-haired mother. The girls and others in the room are also laughing. Lena wipes her eyes and says something to the doctors. Kojo doesn't know if she is crying from happiness or worry or relief, or all of it and more.

She hasn't even bothered to sit down, just holds on.

# Acknowledgments

I must thank my family, starting with KK, and also my children, my parents, my sister, brothers, sister-in-law and brother-in-law; I couldn't have done this without you. It really feels like, together, we have started to build something creative. It is wonderful to know it will keep going through many more books set in different landscapes, time periods and with varied and diverse characters.

Special thanks go to my father, as well as Renee Miller, Emily Steadman, Rachel Booth, Tejshri Shah, Flora Spiegel and Mary Chesshyre, my editor, for their useful reactions to drafts. You helped to shape my thinking and improve the writing, and I really appreciate your time.

I would also like to thank my readers, those who have reached out to me in person, online, or through other forums to tell me what my writing has meant to them. Thank you for taking a chance on my books, for carrying on reading until the last pages, and for telling other people about them. It means so much to an author to know that the words we have written are going places in the minds of others, all over the world. Personal recommendations are so important, and it's the best compliment you can give an author.

If you liked this book, leaving a review on Amazon, Goodreads, or any other book site is so helpful to reach new readers. Also, sharing the book with book groups, requesting it from your local library, and staying in touch through my mailing list all helps to build momentum and keep me going through the difficult times and early drafts.

If you would like to join my mailing list for emails about future books, creative writing and photography, I would love to hear from you at

www.abkyazze.co.uk

# About the author

A.B. Kyazze is a British–American writer and photographer. She spent two decades writing and taking photographs around the world in conflicts and natural disasters – in Africa, Asia and the Balkans. Her photographs and non-fiction work have been published in travel magazines, *The Huffington Post*, *The Washington Times*, *The International Review of the Red Cross*, and by Oxfam, Save the Children, the British Red Cross, and the Humanitarian Practice Network of the Overseas Development Institute.

*Into the Mouth of the Lion*, A.B. Kyazze's debut novel, was published in May 2021. She has also published the *Humanity in the Landscape* photography book series, and a number of short stories, articles and book reviews. Today, she lives in southeast London with her young family. There she writes, mentors other writers, runs a freelance editing business, and facilitates creative writing workshops for children in schools and libraries.

Please stay in touch about creative writing and photography:
www.abkyazze.com     Twitter: @abkwriting     Instagram: @abk_writing

# Also by A.B. Kyazze

*Into the Mouth of the Lion* (2021)
*Humanity in the Landscape* photography series (2012)
*Conflict & Peace*
*Rural & Urban*
*Work & Play*

*Learning from the City: British Red Cross*
*Urban Learning Project Scoping Study* (2012)

*At a Crossroads: Humanitarianism*
*for the Next Decade* (Save the Children, 2010)

*In the Face of Disaster* (Save the Children, 2008)

*Legacy of Disasters: The Impact of Climate*
*Change on Children* (Save the Children, 2007)

*Beyond the Headlines: An Agenda for Action to Protect*
*Civilians in Neglected Conflict* (Oxfam, 2003)

*Angola's Wealth: Stories of War and Neglect* (Oxfam, 2001)

Lightning Source UK Ltd.
Milton Keynes UK
UKHW011337290722
406568UK00002B/107